Robert Smeaton has been self-employed in Estate Agency and Surveying, as a Chartered Surveyor since 1980 in North Cumbria. He has over 35 years of experience, and has seen at first hand the change in the nature of Estate Agents and the causes of the boom and bust housing market, with the consequent periods of inflation, deflation and rise and fall in housing market activity. The author is married with three children.

Dedicated to my wife Marie, for putting up with the 'Agony and the Ecstasy' of Estate Agency.

Robert J. Smeaton

THE REAL ESTATE
AGENT & THE GREAT
CONSPIRACY THEORY

AUSTIN MACAULEY
PUBLISHERS LTD.

A CIP catalogue record for this title is available from the British Library.

ISBN 9781786120632 (Paperback)
ISBN 9781786120625 (Hardback)
ISBN 9781786120649 (E-Book)

www.austinmacauley.com

First Published (2016)
Austin Macauley Publishers Ltd.
25 Canada Square
Canary Wharf
London
E14 5LQ

Acknowledgments

To Christine 'Fingers' Nelson who with me saw the book
form over many years of loyal employment and
observation.

And to all those who've helped in its production.

Contents

FOREWORD

Most of you will probably not realise how much severe disruption the High Street Banks' lending policies, since they were allowed into mortgage lending, have caused to the housing market. The policy of increasing lending ratios to income caused high inflation and then by reducing those ratios, negative equity in the late '80s and early '90s, with similar mistakes being made in 2002 and 2008. Now the Credit Crunch and the change of lending criteria, whereby the lender requires large deposits before the banks will lend, has affected and continues to affect the British publics' ability to move house. In 1988, two million housing transactions took place in England and Wales, representing 15% of the housing stock, with everybody moving every 7 years. In 2006, near the peak of the last so called boom, only 1.4 million transactions took place, representing 5% of the existing housing stock with everybody moving every 17 years. Since the Credit Crunch, the transaction levels have dropped to as low as 600,000 p.a. We were made prisoners in our own homes, unable to move and get on with our lives.

What is less understood by the public is how the banks and other institutions have influenced Estate Agency, Surveying and Mortgage Broking, in order that the profit from housing transactions goes to large corporate firms and the City, rather than local professionals.

Things simply are not what they seem. The new Help to Buy Scheme recently brought in by the government, is heralded as help for First Time Buyers. Houses sell, not on their own merit, but by what the people trying to buy them can afford. With a higher percentage loan in effect provided by the government (or you the tax payer), the First Time Buyer will incur a reasonable mortgage rate and pay a price that builders could not achieve, due to the banks' lending policies and, the latter requiring the first time buyer to have a large deposit. Nobody is telling these First Time Buyers that once they have bought the house it is no longer new, and the next person coming to buy it will not get the same assistance. They will be trapped in that house which is worth less than they paid for it as soon as they turn the key, unless the lending criteria changes. The corporate builders will have sold their houses, by means of a government backed scheme, not available to the next purchaser. The Real Estate Agent asks the question, 'Why is the Scheme to provide 20% of the purchase price only available on New Build'? On an existing house, the Scheme merely guarantees the 20%. result; the banks will give a good rate on new build, (comparable to pre credit crunch levels) as they say they are lending 75% but a punitive rate on existing homes, as they consider they are lending 95%. The corporate builder has been bailed out at the taxpayer's expense. Many first time buyers who would have bought existing homes have been lured to new build out of necessity, further blighting the recovery of the general housing market, as they are not buying from existing home owners who could then move on.

By taking you through the house selling and buying process and by other random chapters, I hope to show you what you should expect from your Agent and the negative effect the practices of modern estate agency largely influenced by the financial institutions, has had on the fluidity of the housing market, and how the policies of the institutions has been about profit at the expense of the British home owning public.

Chapter 1

Big Bang

There can be few professions that have had more upheaval over the last 40 years than Estate Agency. Not to mention the credit crunch, there has been legislation such as the Property Misdescription Act 1991, the Estate Agents Redress Act 2007 and the aborted introduction of Home Information Packs, (which had some merit but would always slow the sale process down not speed it up) and, the advent of Rightmove and other internet portals with all the practical advertising and cost implications. However, the change that really made the difference was the Estate Agents Act of 1979.

Before this time, banks and other institutions had realised that Estate Agency was a meeting place on the High Street, where the public made probably their biggest financial decision, with regard to borrowing money to buy a house, disposing of money when they had sold a house (hence existing Probate Departments in banks), and taking out life insurance to ensure payment of the mortgage on death (at that time endowment mortgages were in vogue). It was around this time that the seeds were being set for institutions to buy into Estate Agency and lo and behold, within the provisions of the Estate Agents Act 1979 were hard rules on the 'qualification' of offers. The corporate companies that were later to buy into Estate Agency were in some cases to use this provision as their excuse (and this still goes on) to not forward their offers to the vendor, until the potential buyer had seen their 'qualifier'. Their 'qualifier' was, of course, their Mortgage Adviser, who then tried to sell the prospective purchasers often their own mortgage and eventually life insurance products. It is hard not to make the assumption that the actual legislation was tailored to allow the banks and institutions to take advantage of the continued biggest conflict of interest of any professional situation. How as an Estate Agent can you possibly be seen to give impartial advice to a vendor, if prospective purchaser A will use you to arrange the mortgage and life insurance, which will result in you getting a second income from the sale, whilst prospective purchaser B will not, as he already has a mortgage arranged, which means you only get the sale commission for the house sale to purchaser B and no other possible income.

The then Chancellor, Nigel Lawson, cemented the feeding frenzy, by allowing High Street Banks to enter the residential mortgage market, which previously had been the hallowed turf of the mutual Building Societies.

Up until this point apart from some London agencies, in the provinces, the majority of Estate Agents were run by people who were Chartered Surveyors or Incorporated Valuers and Auctioneers. They were qualified professional people and treated the business as a profession, with an understanding that there was a fiduciary relationship (one of trust and care) between

Agent and Client and primarily, the business was run as a profession on the basis of doing the right thing for the client and the money took care of itself. All this was to change and the companies that were about to take over Estate Agency, had a doctrine of running it as a business rather than a profession, putting their own interests first, above the interest of the Client. In years to come, that was to work against them as this, coupled with a misunderstanding of how the market works, led to and caused a dramatic fall in the number of transactions i.e. sales, taking place in England and Wales. This therefore reduced their profitability not only in Estate Agency, but in their core businesses, as they did not lend as much money as they would have done had they not spoilt the market.

As the Banks (along with Building Societies and Insurance Companies) tried to get into every type of business conceivable, their most prominent target was Estate Agency. Their interest at the time was not in the business of selling houses, but in the realisation that there was a cross-selling opportunity. The ability to do this had already been shown by the more 'progressive' multi-branch agencies, particularly in the South of England. I am sure that the majority of Agents conduct a transaction properly, but the fact is that allowing cross-selling and effectively the Agent to be paid by both Vendor and Purchaser, opens up a greater ability and temptation to abuse the situation, and it is the area of financial services where staff are usually targeted. Estate Agency was seen as fly paper for selling mortgage products and Banks and Building Societies and Insurance Companies waded in, paying vast sums of money for core Estate Agencies, who the fees would be twice as much, so they retired earlier than they should and were grateful. For a time, the junior partners muddled through some taking to, but many not, the corporate world. Gone was the ethos of looking after the client, the aim was looking after the business. Accountants ruled as board count (the number of 'For Sale' boards you had on the streets) and market share became the most important issue. If it meant over-valuing a property to get it on the market and keep market share up, do it, it will sell eventually. Those professional people who had stayed in Estate Agency were very quickly being winkled out. Staff training by corporate people literally involved training people to dupe the public. Every house had to be got on the market, whether it was right for the client, no matter what their age or situation. Valuation training consisted of 'what do you think your house is worth Mrs Smith?' Answer: 'well that's what you are here for' Statement: 'well if we got you £100,000 you would be delighted'. The trainee 'Estate Agent' would then be told to gauge the reaction and if they seemed generally pleased, to bring the price down, to say 'if we got you £80,000 you would be a little disappointed'. Again, depending upon the reaction, they would say 'what if we ask £95,000'. Training consisted more of selling other products and very soon, when you went into Estate Agents you were being asked questions about your finances, before being asked what sort of house you were after. The majority of practising residential Estate Agents who were qualified, simply quit the business, unwilling to act in the manner insisted upon by the new breed of bosses, whose arrogance was unbelievable and who hailed from the world of accountancy and that of Financial Services. Agents who commanded incomes of £40-45,000 were replaced by 'trained' personnel earning £8,000 per annum. The profession was being dumbed down. Years and years of experience and understanding, had simply left and a new corporate breed was left spending money like water, on re-branding and training by people who in many cases did not understand the business; they were rushing headlong into calamity. Of The Real Estate Agents, who could have helped them, all but a few had gone with a wave goodbye and a thank you, for the large sums they were paid for their businesses. The institutions, having bought all these Estate Agents and formed these groups, were committed to years of losses by the Banks and Building Societies altering their lending criteria. Negative equity became a feared phase in the early '90s (and now again in the 2000s) but it was largely caused by the Banks themselves, through having lent 4 ½ times salary for a house purchase, which meant people could afford and pay more, then suddenly deciding they would go back to lending 3½ times salary. This meant that the same type of person with the same income coming along, who would have bought the house, but maybe altered his lifestyle, could simply not raise the money. The Lenders caused the negative equity themselves, overnight. People who had paid top price for a property when interest rates were at 8½%, suddenly found that they could not afford the property any longer. (Interest rates had gone to 15% plus). The Banks effectively pulled the rug from under them by not allowing the next person coming along, who could perhaps have afforded it in a different way, to buy it. Clearly because of the higher interest rates, there had to be some adjustment, but the blanket approach was insensitive and probably not totally necessary. In the South of England where there was more disposable income, it was a complete disaster with repossessions rife; in the North it was not quite as bad as the multiple of income to loan was not as large. Unbelievably the mortgage lenders were to do the same between 2002 and

At the turn of the decade, huge chains of agents that had taken millions to acquire were disposed of for as little as £1. General Accident, Prudential, Nationwide to name but a few, got out of that simple Estate Agency business, because they could not do it. It was a business they never properly researched before buying into it, and where they perceived everybody always made pots of money for doing very little and requiring no skill. Huge infrastructures were acquired for virtually nothing (in some cases for £1) and in some of these cases, people who knew about estate agency were put in charge. Some brand names such as Countrywide, Your Move, Reeds Rains and Connells were to make a go of it and they continue to compete with the smaller independent chains and some local Building Society chains. The Financial Services Authority made sure that it was very difficult for people who weren't already mortgage brokers, to become one, so whereas it was easy for mortgage brokers to become Estate Agents, it was not easy for professional Surveyors and Estate Agents to become mortgage brokers. The thing that bonded all these large companies was that they sold financial services and still do and the original conflict of interest situation, that originally brought the institutions into Estate Agency, has been allowed to continue, aided and abetted by the powers that be, given respectability through the Ombudsman Scheme and without a squeak from the Consumers Association. Independent Estate Agents took the stance in many cases 'if you can't beat them, join them' and so the public as a consumer goes into an Estate Agency quietly trying to get the house as cheaply as possible, but has to be 'qualified' and therefore tells a Qualifier (Mortgage Adviser) his income and all his financial details and exactly the amount he can afford. The Vendor sells his house through this Agency which will not only get an income from his fee, but also from the purchaser. There has to be obvious concerns;-

1. Why should a prospective purchaser have to tell an Agent exactly the full amount he can afford, thus weakening his negotiating position, other than that he is good for the offer he makes?

2. Were prospective purchasers who would not take their mortgage through the Company given the same encouragement or opportunity to buy the house, perhaps at a higher price?

It has to be wrong; it is not in the publics' interest. The one-stop-shop has been given respectability because everybody does it. If you are buying, you should not have to tell the Estate Agents Mortgage Adviser exactly what you can afford, strengthening their negotiation stance. You as the public, want a fair deal, you want to know that when you buy and sell, you will be treated fairly. You want to move house and get on with life.

The integrity and knowledge was simply got rid of as referred to earlier, the profession was dumbed down.

By going through the process of buying and selling, I hope to give you an understanding of the wrongs that happen today and the way it would be handled by the Real Estate Agent.

If you are thinking of moving, then the first step is to have the house 'valued'. This should give you the amount of money your house will sell for.

Oh! If only life were so simple.

SECTION I – SELLING A HOUSE

Chapter 2

The Valuation

If you are thinking of moving house, or indeed have decided to sell your property, then the first and most natural stage is The Valuation of the property in question. The American word for Valuation is Appraisal and you will find that the larger British corporate firms have predictably adopted the term Market Appraisal, which has been slightly changed from the American meaning of Appraisal, to mean a general market overview. In many cases, Agents no longer place a value on a property they merely recommend an asking price. In fact, so frightened are they to actually place a value on a property, that many of their contracts will actually state that the asking price is not a valuation. Many companies do not put the valuation/market appraisal in writing, as a written letter could possibly be used against them, if the 'valuation' proved to be so far out that someone could sue for negligence. Having seen the cost to people, because of high valuations, I am amazed that more people do not look into it more closely. The real cost of having a house on the market for a long time is, of course, also human as the one thing that none of us like, is uncertainty. In any event, if a company is not prepared to put a valuation down in writing to you, it simply means they do not have enough confidence in the people they are sending around to value, so why should you?

Rule No. 1 therefore, is that you should not just request an asking price, but a valuation for what your property will sell for within a reasonable period of time and you should ask for it in writing. If they are not prepared to do that, then the reason is self-evident.

You should always remember that for an Estate Agent, the difficulty is not selling a house; the greater difficulty is getting houses on the market. Pundits will advise you to get a number of Agents around to value the property. Whilst this gives you a choice and the chance to meet and view all possible Agents, it also means that valuations are no longer valuations, but pitches to get the property on the market. As one lady Estate Agent I was interviewing said to me, after stating that I had a reputation for under-valuation, 'if I know other Agents are going, I put £50,000 on the top'. If an Agent hasn't got them, he can't sell them and so there is a huge temptation to 'list at any price'. Thus houses sell for a lot less than the initial asking price after a long period of time and often for less than they would have made, had they been more realistically priced to start with.

Particularly in more unique properties, those who get lots of valuations will often be completely confused by the end of it. There is often a massive range of valuations, more particularly in country and village properties, but even on estates where it should be relatively easy. Deciding which is the correct valuation, is really very difficult for the Vendor. Some Vendors don't even care which is the correct valuation, they will simply go for the highest, and link that in with the cheapest fee and it can be an unbeatable formula for the unscrupulous Agent.

You should also differentiate between a valuation and an asking price. I would expect a valuation to be probably given in the terms of a band of say 5% of the property value, to say 10% more in the most expensive and unique properties, where affordability is not so much linked to mortgage availability; a purchaser with capital may be prepared to pay above the general level.

It may be, of course, that all your valuations concur, but what you are also looking for in any Agent, is a thoroughness of approach. If an Agent only relies on a cursory look and a valuation 'off the top of his head' without recourse to comparables and research, then he will simply not get it right all the time. If an Estate Agent is seeing a big number of transactions in the area, then his knowledge will be greater than those who have not, but even they should in my opinion, give some time to fine tuning the valuation, to make sure they get it right. It is very easy to run through your computer and suddenly good comparables will spring up to the Real Estate Agent. In his office, every house sale is documented and every house measured, in terms of square metres, and given a price per square metre. The correct valuation to start with is so important, as if you think that your property is worth more than it is from the very start, then decisions will be made during the marketing based on a mistaken belief.

To help you decide on the validity of the Estate Agent and the valuations that he produces, I would suggest the following: -

1. As above, always ask for a valuation in writing and not just an asking price.

2. Ask how long the valuer has worked in your area as a valuer.

3. Ask how many properties the Agent has sold in the vicinity, within the last year. (Not just had a board up, actually SOLD).

4. Ask for the comparable evidence used in arriving at your valuation.

5. If he has the comparable evidence, ask how long it took to sell those comparables and how near the asking price did the properties sell for.

6. If your property is an older property, perhaps in need of repair, then ask what defects he has taken into account in arriving at his valuation, and the allowance in terms of money. Whilst Market Valuation does not include a full survey, I would expect a property professional to quickly assess the patent defects and probably some of the latent defects within a property and take them into account. Someone with no structural knowledge simply cannot do this.

Many people will decide which Agent to use, simply on the amount of the valuation and the person that came around and the impression they gave. This is perfectly natural, but in some firms you may never see the Valuer again, as he goes on to the next valuation and you will be dealing with a negotiator, who has the unfortunate task of trying to sell the property at an inflated price. Remember, regardless of what is said on the day, of the greatest importance is how the firm deals with the sale and how they attend to the transaction process. It is also far better if all interested parties can be present at a market appraisal/valuation. I am sure that in many cases, if both partners were present, the choice of Agent would be different as the transcript from what the Agent said, from the partner who was present to the partner who wasn't, understandably may miss the most important points.

Lastly, people often say that a valuation is what you can get for the property. I ardently disagree with this, having been in the position many times, of trying to re-sell a property where the vendor paid far too much for it, when he or she bought it. I believe a 'theoretical valuation' is a figure that is achievable again, within a reasonable period of time. In other words, there is a depth of market and there is a level of affordability amongst the public, to allow that sale price to be achieved again. With any property, it should be remembered that there is always the chance of a 'lucky hit'. Put a high asking price on it and somebody pays it, but if that sale goes wrong, is there anybody else around to pay it again? The more unique the type of property, the more chance there is of a 'lucky hit' being achieved: that one person with the affordability, who falls in love with the house or its location, and pays it, that special bungalow or flat, close to the town centre and is needed by an elderly person with capital. The real

Estate Agent will understand that and recognise that type of property and will advise the client accordingly.

Having established that you need 'a theoretical value', so you then know a base figure on which to calculate your future purchase or aim, and then, you need to decide on an asking price for the property. When the Real Estate Agent visits a property, the questions he asks are 'have you seen a property that you wish to move to?' and 'What are we trying to achieve?' This quickly will tell him why you, the vendor have got him there for. The reasons for wanting a valuation and the reasons for moving are, of course, numerous.

- Yes, we have seen a house we want to move to,
- No but we need a bigger house,
- We need to move with our job,
- We are getting divorced and need to sell,
- The house is too big,
- We need a bungalow,
- We need to be able to walk into town,
- We want to move nearer the grandchildren,
- We cannot afford the mortgage,
- We are selling to raise some capital for a business,
- This is my parents' house and they left it to us; it is empty and deteriorating.

There are many more reasons why people wish to sell their houses, but unless the Agent asks the question and establishes why, and tailors the advice to your reason for moving, then he is not a thinking agent. If you are trying to buy a property further down the village, which you think is reasonably priced, there is no point in putting a high asking price on your own and endangering its ability to sell and losing the house you are after. The Real Estate Agent understands that the job is about moving people and whilst you always want to get the highest price possible, it can be about getting the highest price at a particular point in time, to enable something else to happen. If you have been left a house, you may well feel that you should put a high price on it and wait for that purchaser to come along who is prepared to pay it. The Real Estate Agent will also point out to you the dangers of that, i.e. an empty property deteriorates, costs money in terms of repairs and can also cost in terms of council tax and other outgoings, such as heating an empty house.

Where your property is and the type of property, also affects the wisdom of a high asking price. If you live in an area where essentially people move within it, with little inward movement, then if you place a high asking price on a property and you don't achieve it, you can end up very much worse off. You do not have new people coming into the area and the locals know it has been on the market for a long period of time. The Real Estate Agent will advise you on the implications of pricing, but there are basically three situations: -

1. Place a very high price on the property with a view to coming down.

This is the method widely adopted by the majority of Agents and very often for the reasons noted above of getting the properties onto the market. When people say 'you can always come down in price' the reply is 'but you can't come down if nobody's looked at it'. Modern Agency can be a very easy job; the agent puts a high price on a property to get it on the market, puts it in the paper with that high asking price and nobody rings, because effectively the price has killed the initial marketing. Where you are most likely to have a 'lucky hit' is where the property is unique, or is in a unique location. Thus if you have a beautiful position high on a hill in the Cotswolds, then to rule out the property making a high price, is rather more difficult than on a semi-detached in downtown suburbia. However, if a property sells well, nine times out of ten it sells early and not after a long period of time. With high asking prices, there is the possibility that if it does not sell, you could end up a lot worse off than had you priced it more realistically in the first instance.

2. You have the theoretical value of your house and you agree to place an asking price within 5% - 10% of that figure.

If you do that, then because you are pricing within peoples' general affordability, i.e. near its theoretical valuation level, then you will get viewings. The Real Estate Agents office will be busy because it is arranging and doing what is necessary to get people around the property. Recently, people have got used to the idea that vendors will have to accept a lot less than the asking price. This is because they are always told to ask too much. If you price realistically you don't drop the price and you simply don't have to, because people can afford it and the offers start to come. As you want to sell the house, the purchaser wants to buy. You have priced at the level of general affordability and 90% of buyers will pay the most they can afford for that property. If that was not the case, most would buy something better. You should ask your Agent to ask for 'Offers in the Region of' and not a fixed asking price. Then he is not guilty of misdescription if the eventual sale price exceeds the initial asking price. Thus, if you get a number of parties interested, the Agent will get interest, and counter offers, but we will deal with this later.

If your house requires extensive modernisation and when improved would have a value of say 25% in excess of its current level, the asking price can exceed the value by a greater percentage than the normal 5% - 10%, as those looking will need to be able to afford up to the asking price, and they will need to spend up to that amount on the price and improvements. Those buyers who can do improvement works themselves, can afford more than those who would have to employ tradesmen.

3. The other method is to actually put the property on low to get interest. Some will see this as wrong and unfair on prospective purchasers, but what it actually does is allow the property to find its level, within a quick period of time. It must be remembered that pricing is only critical in a normal market if you over-price and stop people going to the property. If you have a property that is likely to create interest, then pricing it around the theoretical valuation, should result in a lot of interest. With some properties you simply need to get people inside. With properties that appear small from the outside or have fantastic views, 'you need people inside looking out, rather than outside looking in'. Very quickly, competition can result and

what happens is that once people have seen a property, it stops being about money and starts being about a home. Let's use a general affordability level of £100,000. If you price it at £135,000, the people who would be interested at £100,000 don't bother to look because they don't think they have a chance. If you price is at £105,000 or say at £115,000, then they think they may be able to get it and will go and look. Once they have seen the property, it suddenly stops being about what they can afford and becomes something tangible, a home. This doesn't happen if you over-price to start with and stop people looking. Further, you have put the property on the market and you get an 'initial push'. If you over-price, you kill it. If you price realistically then you can sell on that push and sometimes having got people involved, they will find extra monies from elsewhere, cash in a pension or borrow £10k or £15k from Mum & Dad. Other people offering gives confidence in the value and counter offers can result in the price being above the initial starting point.

The decision on where to start, which is a good way of putting an asking price, depends on what you are trying to achieve, and how quickly you need to achieve a sale. It depends upon the type of property and whether there are others around in the area like it. It depends upon its general initial appearance, whether an unflattering first impression can be overcome, or whether the views can only be appreciated from within. It depends upon market conditions and whether the Agent thinks there are enough people in the area to be interested and create competition at that particular point in time. The more people the Real Estate Agent has, or thinks he will have, the more comfortable he or she will be in placing it a bit lower, with a view to getting competition. Thus the Real Estate Agent will look at the whole situation and a lot of consideration will be given as to where you place the asking price and why. The initial setting of a price, 'the starting point' is perhaps the most critical point of the entire house sale. If the Real Estate Agent thinks the property is likely to appeal to a lot of people, he knows that by pricing at a sensible level, a level where there is a degree of affordability, he will get a number of people interested and offers, and counter offers will result in the property finding its own level.

Some prospective clients do not become clients, because they think an Agent or Valuer did not think their property was worth what they thought. The Real Estate Agent tells the prospective client the truthful theoretical value; suggests a range of asking prices dependent upon the circumstances, discusses the pros and cons, and then takes the clients instructions. In other words, he tells them what he truly thinks and then does as he is told by the client. What he does not do is tell the prospective client what he wants to hear, and as happens so much today, then let them find out by a long marketing period that it was not worth what they thought. If he takes it on at a higher level the client wants, the Real Estate Agent does everything to make the clients' aspirations come true, and if a prospective purchaser asks, in those situations, whether the Real Estate Agent thinks the asking price is high, and what the property is really worth, the retort is simple; 'the asking price is XXX, you put an offer in of what it is worth to you'. There is never any compulsion for an agent to disclose what he believes the value to be, unless it is absolutely in the interests of his client.

Chapter 3

The Process: Choosing Your Agent

From an Estate Agent's perspective, the process of selling a house briefly comprises the following elements:

The Valuation/Market Appraisal, The Valuation & General Advice, Being Instructed and entering a contract of employment with the Vendor, Preparation of Sales Particulars and the proposals relating to advertising and marketing. Then there is internal office organisation relating to the management of the proposed sale, arrangements for viewings, negotiation and taking offers and maximising the price (to some Agents who act as mortgage brokers, broking the mortgage, so giving mortgage advice), accepting an offer and instructing solicitors. Thereafter, keeping in touch with the solicitors and the purchasers, monitoring progress and assisting the process where necessary, and being paid on completion of the sale. Job done!

In order to choose an Agent, you the vendor, have met a number of Agents possibly at the first stage only, the valuation/market appraisal and general advice stage. You will no doubt have had fees quoted but very little will have been discussed about the actual organisation and selling process of the individual agent you intend to instruct. A decision very often is often made purely on the initial impact of the individual concerned and the valuation advice and in many cases, the 'Valuer' will have nothing else to do with the actual process, and yet it was probably on his or her appeal that the decision was made. The fact is that whatever anybody says on the day, it is actually how the company performs during the whole process, as briefly outlined above and you are simply not going to know how generally an office performs, from a one-off meeting with an individual. Many Estate Agents are instructed because they offer the cheapest fees. This, however, makes some overriding and very simplistic assumptions:-

1. THAT ALL AGENTS ARE THE SAME AND THE SERVICE THEY PROVIDE IS THE SAME

2. THEIR ABILITY AND WILLINGNESS TO NEGOTIATE OR FIND THE BEST BUYER WHO IS PREPARED TO PAY THE MOST AT ANY POINT IN TIME IS THE SAME. Neither are true.

Let's assume there are two Agents A & B. Agent A is what I would call an introductory agent only and is charging 1%. You have your house on the market for sale at £105,000 and Agent A receives an offer of £95,000. He communicates the offer to you properly in writing and asks you verbally for your response. What do you think? This offer will allow you to proceed and achieve what you are trying for, so you accept.

Agent B is the Real Estate Agent. Charging 1.5% He receives the same offer of £95,000 and communicates this to you in writing and possibly verbally, but Agent B advises you to wait and see if the other parties who have viewed are interested and quickly works on this. We will assume that they are not interested, so then taking into account his valuation, he advises you to offer it back to the purchaser at £100,000, on the basis that he will take it off the market to the offeree but that he will not lose the offeree if he will not pay more. Let us assume that a counter offer is made at £98,000 and you accept. The extra cost of Agent B in terms of commission will be £500 plus VAT, but this is more than covered by the extra £3,000 received in the sale price. The analogy can apply all through the above process that the Agent carries out. If he advertises a property in a more appropriate place, if he carries more staff who have more time to talk to people and give out alternative properties, then overall, he will turn over more properties and sell them for more money.

I therefore suggest that when choosing an Agent, you look at later chapters as to what the Agent should be doing in terms of the work of selling a house and question him or her on some of these points. There are, of course, other ways of trying to get to know how an Agency performs, once they are instructed. You may have friends who have used a particular Agent. Ring them and ask how it went, how was communication and level of care? If you have a Solicitor, ring him and ask which Agents generally appear thorough and give good advice. They know which Agents generally their clients do not mind paying and those they feel did very little to earn their fee. Whilst the Solicitor may have some business attachment to a particular Agent, he is not likely to point you in the wrong direction.

In reaching a decision, you will already have taken into account the thoroughness of the valuer in arriving at his valuation, and asked him/her how he/she arrived at his figure and what comparables he/she used. I would have expected a good Agent to have given you general advice as to the market conditions and the pros and cons of asking prices, etc., as discussed above.

I am always surprised that when people are choosing an Estate Agent, they do not visit the individual offices posing as a potential buyer, (which they will be if they are staying in the area), or indeed as a potential Vendor (which they most certainly are). Ask for details of a particular property and if you are posing as a buyer, the Real Estate Agent will try and engage with you. It is not the general rule that people buy the property they first came in for. If you were to be selling through that company it may be that it was not the property you were selling that was asked for, and I am sure you would like to think that with someone coming into the office, if there was a slight chance that your property may be of interest, they should be given its details. The Real Estate Agent will have given you the details you have asked for, but he will be asking you what sort of property you are after and what area you are looking in. In this day and age, the Real Estate Agent will be accessing their data base, going through their list of properties in a methodical way (not going around the shop with you, as with one client they will end up starting at one end and with another client at the other end and something will get missed in the middle), from a list the negotiator is now well acquainted with. Extra properties will be given to you and this means that that is a Real Estate Agent, who is trying to give the buyer the maximum number of properties that they have on their books that could be of interest, thus giving the vendors the maximum chance of selling. The Real Estate Agent will then take your name and address and will also take details of the type of property you are looking for. Computers allow easy matching and an e-mail address will enable details of any new properties to be sent to you very easily. Being a potential Vendor, I would expect the Real Estate Agent to ask you for a valuation with regard to your own property, and if you have already sold, ask questions as to the progression of your sale.

Then of course there is the question of the mortgage. You will be able to see the emphasis that is placed on this, where many agents are more interested in selling you a mortgage and introducing you to their mortgage adviser, than trying to find you a property. Again you will be able to judge.

Obviously there may be odd times when a front of house sales negotiator is so busy that he cannot do the above, but if he is not asking those questions of people coming into the office on a regular basis, then he is simply not a Real Estate Agent and not pro-active and the office is probably understaffed. They are the type of Agents who wait for everything to come to them, rather than going that extra mile and making things happen and if understaffed, are probably cutting fees.

As mentioned earlier, we have seen the growth of the large companies and the corporate-backed chains. You may feel more comfortable with this type of organisation, or you may feel more comfortable with a privately owned small office chain, which essentially is run by the owner and is in a sense, a family business. Over the years, it has become apparent that whilst the chains prosper in large urban conurbations, the smaller Estate Agents prosper in the market towns. The reason is most probably that the chains are volume businesses and they need a volume of transactions to be profitable and make having an office worthwhile. In large conurbations everything is less personal. In small market towns, everybody knows everybody else and it is more on local reputation and personality that decisions as to who to use are made. There is also a general assumption, I believe, in the conurbations, the bigger the company, the better the service will be. Does corporate business really give better service to its clients? Does it always put the interest of clients first, before its own?

Taking into account all of the above, at the end of the day you, the client, have to be comfortable with who you are dealing with. Remember that the person you have met at the valuation/marketing appraisal is the person who knows your circumstances, has met you and is better able to understand the type of tailored service that you require. He/she is the one that should be helping you achieve what you are trying to achieve. I would expect the Real Estate Agent to be involved in the process of your sale and in touch with you and oversee your sale from start to finish, rather than hand you over to a negotiator who has never met you, and does not understand first hand your requirements, or likely personal needs.

Do you use a firm that is also a Mortgage Broker? If an agent sells a house to a person who will do a mortgage with him he gets paid by both the seller and the purchaser.

Let's illustrate a conflict of interest situation. Let's assume you have Purchaser A and Purchaser B:

Purchaser A is cash and Purchaser B will take out a mortgage brokered by the selling company and also take out life insurance, giving an additional fee income of say £1,000. Which person is the Agent hoping buys the house? Supposing Purchaser A offers £98,000 as his initial offer. If an agent approaches Purchaser B and tells him £100,000 will be acceptable, subject to his mortgage, you the client accept £100,000 but Purchaser A was never given the chance to offer £100,000 or perhaps even more, and is simply told the property has been sold to someone who made a higher offer. I am not saying that every Agent who brokers mortgages acts in this way, but I am equally sure that many do. It is a basic conflict of interest situation and it has been given respectability, because big business does it. The Ombudsman Scheme was dreamed up by the corporate Estate Agents to cover it. If your Agent brokers mortgages, there will be counter arguments of more knowledge as to the purchaser's affordability and qualification of the offer, but the fact very simply remains that if an Agent brokers mortgages, he will get extra monies if one person purchases the house, over another. There is an undeniable potential for conflict of interest and no regulatory or Ombudsman Scheme can cover every scenario.

Lastly, there is a widely held belief that you can be a property agent without knowing anything about the structure of property. Particularly if you have an older house, it is very relevant to ask if there is a Surveyor or property person within the company who could address the situation, if your property has an adverse survey. You should not assume that everything a Surveyor says with regard to defects to a property is correct. Put two Surveyors on the same property and you will get widely differing conclusions, but let's take a typical situation.

We have a property built in approximately 1900 with no damp proof course, but solid floors throughout. The Surveyor reports 'slight rising dampness and the floors should be taken up and inspected for damp rot or timber deterioration'. This is despite the fact there is no sub-floor and it is of solid concrete. A retention is asked for of £5,000 to cover the work and the purchaser wants £5,000 off the asking price. How can you negotiate this situation, unless you have some knowledge of surveying? The Real Estate Agent will ask for a copy of the report or the main items on it, inspect the property himself and come up with a conclusion and thus be in a far better position to negotiate a say £1500 drop in price for the damp course work only. I have just witnessed a report which indicated that the timber framing was put in a position to cover dampness and other mysterious defects to the wall, when in fact it was a barn conversion and the whole of the building was timber framed, within the lining to the external barn walls. The Real Estate Agent has the knowledge of property and its structure and in this instance, we were able to put the purchasers back on track, showing them the flaw was not in the property but in the survey.

The majority of re-negotiations after agreeing a price are due to surveyors down-valuing or coming up with defects that they say require attention, or more likely from an inspection by somebody else altogether, a damp proof course or timber specialist, who only get business if they find fault. How can a sales negotiator with no knowledge of structure, properly re-negotiate and get the best deal for you as a vendor? I hope by now that the 1% quoted by Fast Harry is not looking such a good bet!

Then there is the comparatively recent option of choosing an online only agent as opposed to a more traditional high street agent. Television advertising has in a sense become the some of the online agents' high street, since it has allowed those that do it to get noticed and grow market share very quickly, but at a huge cost. Eventually, that market share will have to be maintained by the service provided and the jury is still out on that one.

If you are considering using an online only agent, then please visit Chapter 9.

You make your choice and commit to an Agent, usually on a basis of sole selling rights, or a sole agency. The next stage is for the Agent to take details and prepare sales particulars and enter a contract.

AGENT'S TERMS

Increasingly, sole selling rights have become the norm, to prevent clever purchasers knocking on a door with a board outside the house, doing a deal with the Vendor direct and getting it a little cheaper, as the Vendor does not then have to pay the Agent's fees, saying he introduced it privately. This is of course, despite the fact that the purchaser saw it advertised in the local paper and/or the For Sale board. We will, of course assume that you are not going to do this and you wish to work with your Agent and expect to pay him a commission. I do not intend to spend too much time on contracts, because at the end of the day they are what they say. Things to look out for are –

1. INITIAL MARKETING PERIOD – This basically means that you cannot move your property to anyone else for a period of time. This is dangerous in the sense that if you fall out with the Agent or have no confidence in him, you are stuck marketing the property with someone with whom you have lost confidence, and further to move Agents, will probably incur a withdrawal fee. Therefore, this period is usually 13 weeks/3 months, but I have seen it as long as 6 months. It makes sense to make it as short as possible, or try and remove it altogether.

2. WITHDRAWAL PERIOD – Some Agents ask for 2 weeks' notice after the marketing period. Again, if you have lost confidence in your Agent then you should be able to leave him at any point in time. I think notice periods should be negotiated to nil.

3. SOLE SELLING RIGHTS OR SOLE AGENCY RIGHTS - These have to be described properly, but the former means that if the house sells, the Agent has to be paid, whether he introduced the purchaser or not.

4. COMMISSION
Make sure you fully understand the commission that is being charged and details of any extras. These may include Viewing Fees, Extra Advertising and
Withdrawal Fees. If there is extra advertising, make sure there is a mandate and you do not pay beyond it.

Remember, the commission charged can be made for you by the Real Estate Agent. Cheap Agents are buying business and, you should ask yourself, why? at 1.5% plus VAT, Agents are not making great profits per office unit.

5. COOLING OFF PERIOD

All contracts have to have a Cooling off Period, which has now been extended. If not the contracts are null and void. If you have any doubts about the contract, consult your Solicitor.

If your Agent is a member of the Property Ombudsman Scheme or a Chartered Surveyor, then he cannot reveal offers, although there is no actual law to say so, it was just put in the Code of Practice of the scheme and Chartered Surveyors followed suit. The Real Estate Agent is of the opinion that he should have the right to negotiate in this manner, if considered appropriate and inserts a clause informing the client, that he reserves the right to reveal offers. (I have dedicated Chapter I in Section I1 to the pros and cons of doing so).

Having made your choice of Agent, it is a question of instructing him and so the process can begin, which is basically as follows:-

IMPROVEMENTS BEFORE SELLING

You want your house to look its best to go on the market. The selling process is about to begin and no doubt you are very busy tidying and finishing off things and decoration; personal pride makes you want to show the house at its best.

How much is done in this regard is really personal and the fact is that how much you do is not up to a professional adviser, but what makes you feel comfortable. You will get widely differing takes on the importance of preparation for viewing. One lady Agent I knew, used to advise people to get an interior designer friend of hers to as it were, 'window dress' the house, before anybody came. The 'percolating coffee brigade' tell me their thoughts, through the programmes on television dealing with the sale of property: how some will claim to have made money from buying a house and selling it, having spruced it up for very little, but probably ignoring the costs of the massive amounts of labour taken to do it. Houses sell because there is need primarily for the location and the size of accommodation offered.

It should always be remembered, that whatever your taste, someone moving into the house may have a different taste and it should also be remembered that nine times out of ten, people will want to put their own stamp on the accommodation. The obvious way is by decoration, but the most changed situations very simply, are the kitchen and bathroom.

Another possible change is either an extension or structural changes within the layout of the existing house. Spending money on such items means that to make it worthwhile, you need to get that money back, and that assumes that the incoming occupant will want what you have done. It sounds like a high risk strategy to me. A situation that sticks in my mind is when a lady sold a house but it took the detail taker about three trips to satisfy her, that her beautiful oak kitchen had been properly described, with every shape, veneer, detail of electrical elegance and excellence explained satisfactorily. The people who bought the property were being moved in to the area by their employee and after six months they were moved out again. Our same detail taker went back and thought she would not have to describe the wonderful kitchen but to her surprise, there was a new and entirely different kitchen in place. The present occupier didn't like it at all and far from being the selling point that the vendor had thought, it turned out to be nothing of the kind.

Whilst tidying and sprucing is in order, the advice the Real Estate Agent would give you with regard to improvements is that the only time it is ever worth spending money on a property that you are considering selling, is when your expenditure improves the first impression which is received when the prospective buyer looks at the property. If by cutting down a long due to be pruned, overhanging bush, or by painting a mould stained wall, or the flaking stone mullions, you give the initial look of the property a lift, then that is worth doing. Once you have people inside the property, they will soon look to alter and design it in their own fashion and the chances of you spending money in the same way as they would, is very slight.

So that's it then, The Real Estate Agent would advise that improvements should be done to improve the first impression of the house, to get people inside it.

Now that you have done that, then it is time to get the sales particulars carried out by your Agent of choice and the Energy Performance Certificate, if your house does not have one, and the process can begin.

SALES PARTICULARS

The idea of Sales Particulars is not just to describe a property but to sell it. The Property Misdescription Act was brought out at about the same time as the corporates were interested in buying out Estate Agents. It may seem ridiculous to think the two were linked, and it probably is, but it certainly allowed the 'yesterday I could not spell Estate Agent, today I are one' to write sales details. You can still see them in the paper, 'detached house, 3 bedrooms, garden' such words as 'elegant sweeping drive, period features' do not come into this type of Agent's vocabulary. The Real Estate Agent is not frightened to paint a picture with words and so it is with advertising and sales particulars: they should be pricking the thoughts of the purchaser, always highlighting what a property has, and the various attributes which may appeal to an individual buyer. On an estate, a corner plot or a slightly larger garden can often make the difference, an open outlook at the front looking down a road rather than straight into another house, an open field to the rear, all these little things build to make a picture of what you are trying to sell. They exist and they make the property more appealing, so they must be brought out. Most Agents' sales particulars are adequate, if only because they are overseen by the vendor, who is able to describe his own property and knows its selling points. However, the Real Estate Agent is the professional and should identify not only what the property has, but the type of person who may be interested in the write up. Modern cameras and printers make high class presentation very possible. These days a floor plan is often a beneficial extra.

If your property has a local occupancy clause, then this should have been referred to as they can vary and do affect value. The property needs to be advertised, subject to this clause.

If you have a property in a block of flats it will almost certainly be leasehold. The length of lease needs to be established. There may be rules relating to keeping a pet, details of the amounts of service charges. Whether the block has a working Freeholders Association or a Management Company should also be established.

The sales particulars should have details of whether the property is freehold or leasehold and I would suggest if it is leasehold, it should also include details of the ground rent, length of lease, etc. If there are service charges then these costs should be readily available, if not on the sales details, they should state which services are available. The Real Estate Agent at this stage involves the Solicitor. Many don't and yet the Property Misdescription Act states that if the Agent does misdescribe a property, he must show that he took active steps to prove what is stated is true. Thus the Real Estate Agent writes to the Solicitors with a list of questions which may include some of the following:

1. The nature of tenure – if leasehold, length left & any maintenance charges

2. The presence of any servient easements affecting the property

3. The presence of a damp proof course guarantee

4. The presence of a timber guarantee

5. The exact age of the property

6. Is there a certificate for cavity wall insulation?

7. Provide a boundary plan showing rights of way and ownership
8. Are there any planning restrictions regarding occupation?
9. Is the property NHBC registered
10. Is the property architect supervised and by whom?
11. Is the property a listed building?
12. Local occupancy clause
13. Has the property had improvements that are likely to require indemnity Insurance, i.e. extensions /conservatories?
14. Other

If your property is an older property, it may have flying freehold and it may have shared rights of access and boundary areas that are not clearly defined. The Real Estate Agent will ask the Solicitor for Boundary Plans together with a marked plan and this should not only show the land owned, but also the various rights of way over it. Ironically, this information was not included, even in the Home Information Pack, (See Chapter 9).

Requests for this information from any potential buyer are bound to arise and it is far better that your Agent has it to hand when the property is marketed. The Deeds need to be inspected by the solicitor, so it is better, generally, that you instruct your Solicitor at the time of commencement of sale, so that the various questions can be answered and incorrect assumptions that may cost time and money later, will be avoided. This will, of course, incur Solicitors costs, even if there is no sale.

ENERGY PERFORMANCE CERTIFICATE

The Energy Performance Certificate is meant to assess your house as to its heat insulation qualities or lack of them. This Certificate has to be ordered at the time of marketing and Exchange of Contracts cannot happen without an Energy Performance Certificate being obtained. Your Estate Agent or Solicitor will almost certainly have a contact. Watch out for Estate Agents charging an extra 'Arrangement Fee'. This type of thing t is affectionately known in the trade (note, not profession) as 'Bolt Ons'

Currently Energy Performance Assessors carry this survey out. Again, I would suggest that if two Energy Assessors went around the same older property, then you would probably get widely differing ratings. Only recently, we have seen a supposedly timber-framed bungalow given an excellent rating for the walls, when in fact it was made of pre-fabricated concrete, with much thinner walls than normal and no insulation. Look critically at the report, particularly where you have an older house.

with many more people and dealing with more viewings. Having difficult bidding situations with three or four people all wanting the same house can be stressful, not only for the purchasers, but also for the Agent. If he has an office full of people all trying to buy the same house, believe me, it takes some sorting out. But he is working for the client and it is his duty to achieve a sale for as much as possible, at that particular point in time and within a reasonable timescale, to allow his client to sell his house and get on with his life and achieve whatever his goal in a timely manner.

In a sense you find out what the house is worth by the marketing exercise. You may have two people at that particular point in time, prepared to get into a bidding situation to acquire it and pay more than the theoretical valuation. It does not mean the theoretical valuation was wrong, it just means two people at that particular point in time, wanted it. 'Ah but a house is worth what somebody will pay'. I disagree with that statement and have been told it many times. I disagree with it, because the number of times I have seen people pay the theoretical value plus £20,000 and then have had the job of re-selling the house and not being able to get it back because they paid too much. There is the theoretical value and then there is what you can get at that particular point in time. The Real Estate Agent realises that there is nothing like competition to achieve a good price on a house. To the prospective purchasers, having someone else interested is almost like having a free valuation. It gives confidence in the offer they are placing on the property, because someone else is prepared to pay it, or very close to it. There is this idea that you have to place a high price on the property and you can always come down, but you cannot come down if nobody has looked at it! How many times have you seen properties sell by public auction (I stress not re-possessions) but say country cottages on a hillside with lovely views, selling at auction and making fantastic prices? Did the auctioneer start high, no, the bidding started low and that competition resulted in the property making a high price and possibly above the theoretical valuation. I have sold many properties by auction and people have come to me afterwards and said 'I was only prepared to offer £X, but when I saw how many people were interested, I went to £X plus £20,000'. The name of the game, therefore, is to get as many people to the property as quickly as possible and the Real Estate Agent does this by co-ordinating all his marketing efforts, (newspaper advert, internet, mailing list, etc.) so that as many people as possible find out at the same time. To this end, I am personally reluctant to tell people of a property that is coming onto the market before we have carried out our marketing, even if I know they are very likely to be the buyer and I prefer to tell them, 'I may have something coming on that will suit them' rather than tell them where it is and what it is. The reason for this is that if they view the property say 10 days before you are ready to market and advertise, etc., they put an offer in and you don't yet have any idea what sort of response your marketing will bring. I can hear people say 'well sell it to them, if you get the offer and it is enough, sell it'. You can of course do that, and there may be times when it is appropriate, i.e. perhaps if somebody does not have a quick offer then they are going to lose the property they are trying to buy, or perhaps if you have a buyer you think will pay over the value, and the enticement is if you pay £X, it won't go on the market. However, it does mean you have not tested the market, you have not found out whether there are more people interested and you have not built the price up, as can happen with good negotiation and offer and counter offer.

The marketing exercise, therefore, means that adverts are placed in the local paper, the property is put onto property portals such as Rightmove and such other websites the Agent uses, and most important of all, the mailing list that the Real Estate Agent has, is put out to coincide with that advertising. It is amazing that many agents do not use Mailing Lists and expect people to find out from the paper or the internet. They do not contact the very people who have made an effort to go around all the agents, go into their offices and register their interest in trying to purchase that particular type of property. When agents do send out the details, they are often criticised for sending out the wrong details. Clearly there are boundaries but the Agents Mailing List should try and expand the prospective purchasers' requirements, as many times, people buy a property, most particularly in an area they did not originally think of. The good agent will have a number of people who he knows are strong buyers and will try and contact them personally. The Real Estate Agent knows that his business relies on getting properties to sell and he will most certainly contact people locally, who could use his agency and have a property to sell. We will discuss later that this need not be terminal in someone's ability to purchase, and in any event, their interest can be used to bolster the price. At the very least, those people should know that the type of property they are interested in is coming to the market as it is amazing how money can be found. The idea then is to get people to the property and if people see it, you will find out what it is worth. That said, you don't necessarily accept the first offer that comes along; other people are viewing. It is here that communication is essential. The Real Estate Agent knows that if people place an offer and don't get a result, or are not kept informed as to what is going on, then they start thinking they will not get the property. Once they start thinking this, human nature decrees that they start thinking of reasons why they don't want it. Thus it is necessary to put a time on it. 'Thank you for your offer, we have other viewings taking place and we will come back to you in five days'. The Real Estate Agent will stress that he will not sell it over their heads and will come back to them if there is any other movement within that time. This means the offeree relaxes. They forget about it until after the Monday, whereas if you do not give them that timescale, they think you will be coming back to them every day and when you finally do come back to them, they are often disillusioned.

In some properties, the marketing exercise can actually involve putting a low initial asking price. In all cases, the asking price should be quoted as Price Region, or asking price Offers in the Region of. Putting a fixed price can involve difficulty with misdescription, if the price gets bid up. I wish I had a pound for every time somebody has said to me 'my house is like a Tardis, it is so much bigger than you think from the outside'. My standard reply to this is, "yes, we need people inside looking out rather than outside looking in." This can also be particularly true of properties that have views. Essentially, therefore, if you put an asking price on the property, a price that the property may eventually make, people will not look at it, because they don't realise what it has. Always remember, once people have viewed, it stops being just about money and starts being about a home and people will find extra monies from somewhere. In terms of asking price, it is not where you start but where you finish that is important.

To a point, photographs and the internet have helped with this, but I can assure you that there is nothing like internal inspection and even with the best will in the world, photographs cannot always convey a property's atmosphere and, in fact, can be detrimental. I wonder how many people have looked at a property on the internet and dismissed it, one that had they viewed, would have liked. We will never know.

For this reason, it is often worth not stating the price in the paper, but putting say 'Price on Application' or 'Offers Invited'. The Real Estate Agent actually does this quite a lot and he is pilloried for it. The buying public will often say we do not look at a property if it does not have a price on it. The reply is, we are not working for you, we are working for the Vendor and we feel that this is the best way of doing it. People say they will not deal with an Agency that does not put prices in the paper. They will, if they are truly looking!

In most cases, I believe that if people are genuinely interested in a house, they will take the trouble to ring up and enquire what the asking price is. As you can imagine, this means a huge increase in workload for the Real Estate Agent. He actually has to talk to people! When the Real Estate Agent places a property on the market and puts 'Price on Application', people will ring in to find out what the price is. His staff record that an enquiry was made and whether details were sent or a viewing was arranged. If you have a lot of enquiries and no viewings when people are told the price, it tells you that the price is putting people off. If details are going out and viewings are being arranged, then you know that the price is encouraging people to look. This information is invaluable because it affects how the Real Estate Agent will handle offers. If he gets an offer early and he is getting a good reaction to the price, then he knows to hold on to the offer and stall the person who has offered. If he receives an offer and has had an adverse reaction, he may then feel that the best way forward is to put it back to that person at an increased price and try and do a deal. If a price is put in the paper and you get no reaction and no interest in the property, you do not know whether the price has killed it or there is just no interest. If you put 'Price on Application' and you get no interest you can at least say to the vendor, it isn't the price, because nobody has enquired about it. The advantage of a low asking price and an offer and counter offer system is that it gives you flexibility. If you have a property that needs to be viewed internally, then you can price it at a level, and expect offers and bidding, so that it will arrive at its own level. You may say 'I don't like that system and find it very stressful'. Yes, it is and it is equally stressful for the Estate Agent, however the alternative is what you have now, which is high prices placed on properties and them selling after months/years, as opposed to weeks. If a property takes years even months to sell, very simply your chains don't work and you have the situation you have now; reduced transaction levels and Agents saying you have to sell your house first, because every house is priced so high and takes so long to sell, that chains don't work. Not only does it allow for speed and flexibility, it actually achieves higher prices. The reason is simple, because once people have viewed a property and 'fall in love' with it, they will go further than they originally intended. If an Agent does not like the bidding system then there is nothing to stop them asking for Best and Final Offers, (although it is my observation, that most purchasers dislike that system even more) and Agents start it too soon, not having built the price and starting the Best and Final situation from a higher platform.

I fully accept that there may be times when an asking price at the high end of a reasonable pricing band is the best way forward. In recent years, in some areas, it has been impossible to get competition, very simply because so few people are moving. Where you have properties that are perhaps unlikely to appeal to many people, then if you don't think you can get competition, you possibly have to begin from a higher starting point. However, in normal market conditions, marketing hard and getting as many people to the property as possible through your marketing, not discouraging people by an asking price well in excess of the property's value, more often than not, will result in the best achievable price at that point in time. The Real Estate Agent will build on the interest and oversee in an understanding and communicative manner, the offer/counter offer that occurs. The property will realise its level at that point in time, within a reasonable timescale. If you have under-priced the property then the viewers will soon tell you, because they will offer for it. I am continually told that people are knocking prices down. That is because the initial asking price is too high and well beyond the affordability of the purchaser, who wishes to purchase. Remember houses sell at levels not through what the house offers, but by what potential purchasers can afford. It doesn't matter what accommodation a house has, if the prospective purchasers cannot afford it, then they cannot pay it. If you ask a proper asking price, then you will find that as you want to sell it, the prospective purchasers want to buy it and they will therefore go to the maximum they can afford and not knock you down hugely from your proper asking price. I would estimate that something like 80% of houses sell for the most the purchaser can afford. Otherwise, they would buy something better.

Many Agents, particularly in the capital, sell to a fixed asking price with a price of £500,000. My understanding of the law is that this precludes the price going beyond this. Why an Agent should put himself under that pressure, I do not understand. I do understand, that particularly in the capital, there is tremendous competition for property. It is easier, therefore, to say Vendor 1 offered the asking price and we accepted it. Always remember that the Agent makes his money out of turning over property, not getting £10,000 more here and there. The Real Estate Agent believes it is his obligation to get as much money for you as possible in a balanced way, and asking for 'offers in the region of', allows flexibility, and the property legitimately can realise in excess of the price guide.

The Real Estate Agent is often told, particularly by people from the South, that they don't like this offer/counter offer, they don't like 'gazumping'! The Real Estate Agents retort is automatic; 'gazumping' originated in the south, as Agents sell to a fixed price and then get higher offers, because they have not tested the market. We sort it out. Test the market and then accept an offer.

ADVERTISING

LOCAL NEWSPAPER ADVERTISING.

Whilst local people will look and come to the office, it is still true to say that the local newspaper is a vital tool to the Estate Agent. Local bespoke property papers are another possibility and some agents in some areas have co-operated in using a local property paper, rather than placing properties in the local newspaper. Personally I prefer to support my local newspaper, but your property will have to be advertised in whichever medium is available to you. Advertising in a local newspaper is more important where interest is likely to be limited to the local market. In other words, people move within the vicinity at various stages of their lives and stay within the local area i.e. from a First Time Buyers Flat, to Larger Family House, to larger still Family House, to Smaller Bungalow, to Retirement Flat. The fact is that people still read the local paper and many still use it as their first port of call. The older the person the more likely this is to be the case, and the more the internet will take over with the demise of the current older generation. Despite the internet, always bear in mind that the size of an Agency's advert and number of new properties coming to the market with him, has an impact upon the perception of the market share and success of that Agency. It does not necessarily mean however that it offers the best service.

NATIONAL ADVERTISING

There are places where people want to live from outside of the area such as National Parks, country areas on the outskirts of towns and places of Outstanding Natural Beauty. All these attract people from substantial distances. In these areas some 'local papers' are actually sent many miles to names and addresses, simply for their property advertising content. If you do have a property in this type of area, then take note, although the internet is making this happen less nowadays.

Once upon a time when Estate Agents were Real Estate Agents and acted for the good of the client, advertising was paid for separately. In other words, the Agent advertised the clients' property and the client paid for the cost of advertising. Remember that Agents were trustworthy people: they charged it at cost and because the Agent was not paying for the advertising, he would advise the client where the advertising should go in the best interest of selling although I would accept there is a situation where an agent could advertise the property to 'bolster his own standing'.

In the late '70s/early '80s, businessmen started to get into Estate Agent as opposed to professional people and the sales gimmick was 'all-inclusive fees – no sale no fee', so if your house didn't sell, you didn't get a bill for the advertising. This understandably took off, but effectively what it means is that immediately you and the Agent are on different sides, as the advertising is coming out of his pocket not yours. Therefore, you do not necessarily get the advice as to where the property should be advertised, apart from the local newspaper where the Agent gets kudos and can negotiate discounts, etc. You will find that some agents have a policy of local newspaper advertising and the website completely covers national advertising. Thus if you have a nice retirement bungalow in the Northern Lake District where I practice, the assumption is made that somebody at retirement age in the North East, where an awful lot of people come from to the Lake District for a change of lifestyle, will be looking at the internet. Some will and some won't and some retirement or second home properties, placed in a North East newspaper, yield excellent results. If you live in a National Park or have a house with something unique to offer, then it is well worth thinking where the type of person might come from to buy your property, second home or retirement home, etc. and ask your Agent to advertise your property in the appropriate newspapers and magazines. The Real Estate Agent will do this for you, but many Estate Agents won't or will try and discourage you, simply because it is more paperwork, more accounting, etc. If you are looking for competition, it only takes one extra prospective purchaser to make a big difference to the eventual sale price. The more you cast your bread upon the water, particularly for an unusual type of property, the better.

THE INTERNET

All Agents now have a website and almost all Agents subscribe to some sort of property portal. At the present time, there is one dominant portal and there are battles going on with other slightly lesser subscribed portals, all aiming to be the best, which will unfold, no doubt. It is clear that those seeking property from outside of an area are now greatly advantaged by the ability to access information on the internet. I would say that this form of advertising is particularly useful to those looking to move from a distance, from outside of an area rather than within it. However, the drawback is that Agents do not have the same contact with prospective purchasers. We see many cases where people say they dismissed a certain property, viewed on the internet, but when they call into the office, they become of the opinion that it may be suitable after all. The ability of agents to sell alternatives is denied somewhat as well, as prospective purchasers look on the web and the Agent does not meet them, or talk to them to offer other ideas.

THE MAILING LIST

Today, prospective purchasers are referred to as Applicants. These Applicants are people who have taken the trouble to contact an Estate Agent's office and leave their details, because they are looking to buy a house. They may even have called into the office. It is therefore essential that the properties coming onto the market, including yours, are matched to these people and the details sent by post or e-mailed out. Some Agents will come with a list of people they say are interested in buying your property, to try and get it on the market and then never actually send it to them. Some Agents say that the cost of postage and time taken, means they don't bother, but that is because they do not update their applicant list. An applicant list needs updating every 3 to 6 months and any person who does not need to be kept on it, should be taken off. This means that the Real Estate Agents list is updated, gets a response from the applicants and is therefore productive. Speaking to an Agent recently, I asked if they sent a mailing list and they said they did not think it was worth it, as people would see the property advertised on Rightmove. This is simply lazy estate agency. We recently contacted two prospective purchasers by telephone, made appointments and both purchasers offered, with this property realising in excess of the asking price with our company. This is pro-active estate agency. It is about making sure that potentially interested parties known to the Agent are informed of the newly marketed property, rather than them finding out through their own devices. All the above are the means by which an Estate Agent can market from when a property is initially placed onto the open market. If you are taking the low price option as discussed, then it is essential that it is done absolutely simultaneously, but if you are taking the high price option, then it may be felt best to stagger the advertising a little. It should always be remembered that a property sells itself; the job of the Agent is to get as many people to it who might be interested and as quickly as possible. It is easier to judge whether a house has reached its full potential in terms of selling price, when a number of people have viewed it.

VIEWINGS

The property is marketed and the first people have shown interest. This may be via newspaper advertising, the internet, the mailing list undertaken we hope, by the Estate Agent, or from telephone calls from the Agent to prospective buyers, or from the telephone calls from those people who are really looking hard. Perhaps they are living in rented accommodation, waiting anxiously for the right property to come along, for that extra stability in life that only acquiring a house of your own, in an area you like, decorating it and making it yours can give.

The situation will usually fall into the following categories:

1. The property is fully furnished and you are in occupation.

2. The property is fully furnished but you are generally not in occupation

3. The property is unfurnished and unoccupied.

In the United States, viewing will always be accompanied by the Realtor. Of course the difference is the commission. The vendor will have paid 7 – 10% of the sale price by the time he is finished; rather more than the 1% - 1.5% charged by estate agents in this country. It is the case in this situation that most agents will ask you if you are happy to do your own viewings. If you say no, then The Real Estate Agent will most certainly undertake those viewings for you and it is probably best that you leave the house for a period of time. Some vendors like to see who is coming around the property so that they get a feel for the situation. If you elect to show people the property, the Real Estate Agent advises to give them a quick tour through the house, briefly showing the layout and perhaps hidden cupboards and the extras in the kitchen. Show them the outside boundaries and invite them back into the house and let them look around then at their own leisure.

PROPERTY FURNISHED AND OWNER-OCCUPIED.

1. Some people will spend hours, even when not interested. You may get 10 viewings in the first week. That's a lot of hours. If they are interested, purchasers know in the first 15 minutes maximum and dependent upon the size of the property, unless it is a mansion, ¾ hour is ample time for them to view it. The Real Estate Agent would advise you to tell the viewers you have something to do in ¾ hour, but if the property is of interest to them, they can come back another time. Use your discretion, but you can see where I am coming from.

2. If a property has defects then the law was, 'let the buyer beware' i.e. you are selling the property with defects and all. It was a personal thing as to what degree you revealed these defects and not all defects are picked

up by surveyors although you had to answer any questions put to you truthfully. Since October 2013 property professionals and sellers are now exposed to consumer protection from Unfair Trading Regulations 2008.Sellers now cannot hide information of "material importance" to a buyer or tenant. Quite who is going to decide what that constitutes is open to conjecture but already cases have been heard and fines dealt. However, whereas Agents are out on a limb, sellers can take comfort from a case in 2014 that acts as a reminder that the Standard Conditions of Sale Fourth Edition contain a provision that gives effect to let the buyer beware, and it is also possible to include special conditions in a sale contract excluding the sellers liability. The seller gets off and the Agent cops it. That is alright then!

The Real Estate Agents view is that minor defects or jobs that you were going to do, be pointed out as this will give confidence in the remainder of the house. The advice is therefore, if you the Vendors are carrying out the viewings tell them everything about the house, tell them things you were going to do and tell them about boundaries and rights of way, but leave it at that. The aggressive purchaser will try and talk to you about price. Older and vulnerable people can be bullied and intimidated into talking and possibly accepting an offer. Do not talk price under any circumstances. One of the most important functions of the Client/Agent relationship is to give distance between the vendor and the purchaser. If you are faced with someone directly negotiating, you will say and do things that you will regret as soon as they have left, or there is a good chance. Of course, it is your property and it is your prerogative but effectively you are stopping The Real Estate Agent from doing his job, at the most important stage. If someone asks 'how much will you accept' the correct answer is, 'I really do not wish to discuss price. If you are interested, please put an offer to the Agent'. When the Agent receives that offer and is asked 'will it be acceptable' he says, 'I am sorry, I will have to speak to the client'. This gap is essential because it gives everybody time to think; it gives the Agent time to do what he should do before the acceptance of any offer is considered, which is to look at the whole picture and then advise accordingly. I once had a vendor who had four viewings in one afternoon. After three of the viewings he rang me to say he had sold it, to each latest individual, each at a higher offer. You can imagine the mayhem that ensued in our office as the disappointed people found out that their offer had not been accepted and that he had sold it again for a higher price. Do not do it, do not talk price.

UNOCCUPIED FURNISHED PROPERTY.

Practicality dictates that where a property is furnished, but unoccupied, the Agent needs to accompany any viewers. The Real Estate Agent will show the property in the same manner as proposed to the owner/occupier above. I would also expect him to have a pen and paper ready to take down any enquiries or questions to which he does not know the answer. However, he will need to be fully acquainted with the property file, and know the answers to the questions asked of the Solicitor, have copies of boundary plans perhaps showing rights of way, and have details of any special or hidden features of the property. As discussed, to this point there is little to be gained for an Agent from doing viewings. Having got the potential buyer to the house, it will sell itself or not. However, I would expect The Real Estate Agent at this point, to try and connect with all the people who are viewing, and to establish whether this house is suitable or not and if not, exactly what they are looking for and give them alternatives. (I stress only having found that this house is not suitable).

If the viewers need to sell their house, I would expect the Agent to offer a sales valuation, (particularly if the viewers are interested in this house). This is good from the seller's point of view, as if the viewers are interested and their house is valued and they are realistic, it may well be that they purchase or place their house on the market and it is better that the same Agent has control. This gives greater knowledge and understanding of their situation and it makes it easier to simply make things work. If a buyer has cash and is not interested in this property, then I would expect The Real Estate Agent to sell their surveying services. Of course, for those Agents that are mortgage brokers, accompanied viewings give the opportunity to try and get this prospective purchaser in front of the Financial Adviser of their company.

The person who conducts the viewing for the Real Estate Agent will summarize to the negotiators whether or not the property could be of interest to the viewers. If it is a definite no, then this can go on the file, so there is no need for negotiators to waste time chasing that particular viewer. If there are valuations to be arranged, then these will be identified.

THE UNOCCUPIED HOUSE WHICH IS UN-FURNISHED

Where property is unoccupied and unfurnished, there is really little reason for an Agent not to hand the key out and somebody simply allow viewers to look on their own. Whilst I would draw a distinction between maybe large houses with complicated boundaries or lots of hidden extras that need explaining, is it really going to make a lot of difference if a viewer is accompanied around a small two-bedroomed semi-detached bungalow, or a small terraced house? Is it going to make the difference between someone offering and not? Frankly I doubt it. The Real Estate Agent nevertheless will ask the question of the client, 'is it alright to give the key out, or would you prefer accompanied viewings' and I would expect to go along with their wishes. In any event, of course, the advantages to the Agent of accompanying are given above.

The situations where a house is left empty are usually:

1. A probate situation where the occupant has died and the house has been left to their descendants or beneficiaries.

2. The owners have been relocated with a job move and the company required the family to move in the short term and the former occupants are either renting or on company bridging finance.

3. The owners have moved and have enough money to purchase another property without selling their old one, and now own two properties.

4. The property has been a Buy to Let and the owner now wishes to sell.

Where a property is a holiday let then it makes sense in almost all circumstances to keep the furniture in-situ. Normally in a small two/three bedroom furnished holiday let, the furniture can be used as a negotiating point i.e. 'the furniture is available at a separate price to be negotiated'.

What usually happens, for an overall price the furnishings are thrown in, but it is of appeal to a prospective purchaser as he does not have to spend the time and trouble, often from a long distance, looking for the replacements etc. They can start holiday letting at once, thus getting an income immediately.

The Real Estate Agent is often asked the question, whether it is better to empty a house or not.

In the case of probate houses, often the contents are at best tired. It is also apparent that they have been occupied by a person who is no longer alive and whilst this may not be totally material, to some it will have a detrimental effect on the atmosphere of the property. At the end of the day, selling a house is a lot about atmosphere, the initial feel when someone walks into the property. This is obviously overshadowed by bereavement and it can have a negative effect on some viewers. Without any doubt, personal effects should be removed prior to viewing and the house organised and cleared of minor objects. If the furniture is reasonable then there is no reason why it should not stay and it will possibly be of benefit, otherwise clear it.

Likewise, with Buy to Let properties, the same applies in the sense that if the furniture is poor, then clear it. If it is anything like serviceable then keep it in-situ as it may well become a bargaining point and of assistance to those seeking Buy to Let property, since the property is already furnished and it saves them a job. Quality is the key here and it is on that that the decision hinges.

Here the family has been relocated or simply another house has been purchased, then there may well not be a lot of choice in the sense that the furniture needs to go with the family. If the furniture can remain and is in good order, then I would suggest normally it should remain.

FEEDBACK

I think my next comment is going to be one of the most contentious of this whole book, particularly if read by some of my colleagues. On accepting instructions, The Real Estate Agent asks the vendor whether or not they require feedback. He then tries to persuade them not to ask for it, on the basis that if people are interested they will get in touch themselves. Feedback is now the norm and people simply demand it, so he will take their instructions and if they require it will endeavour to supply it. Whilst I would qualify the next statement, feedback is a complete waste of the Agents' time, time that could be better spent pursuing people who may be interested, rather than pursuing people who aren't. If a prospective purchaser is interested in a property, very simply they will contact you. Whenever The Real Estate Agent carries out feedback from the viewing files, with the list of those who have viewed and where the feedback is recorded, it may show entries such as 'Have rung three times and left messages, no reply'. The people who viewed are simply not interested in the property; some will consider that the Agent is hounding them and some simply do not have the courtesy to respond. When you do get hold of them, do you think you get a real reason why they don't want it? They just don't like it. It is a waste of time if done simply for the sake of it. I am not saying that there is not a case where a house has been on the market for a long period of time, to try to get a reason for it not selling, but frankly, usually the Agent does not need to speak to a whole plethora of viewers who may or may not be giving the real reason, to tell his client why that is.

Feedback was brought in by the Corporate Estate Agents. The reason is very simple, you have a contact, you have people, and you have the chance to sell them financial services. Ring them up, it is not about whether they are interested in the property, you know they are not or they would have contacted you. It is to try and get a mortgage lead.

That is why feedback to the extent it is done today started. The Real Estate Agent does not ring people who have viewed and does not consult the viewing file as a matter of course, but does so when he has received an offer. He looks at the list of views and judges who could be interested, sees if anyone has asked to be kept informed of offers, looks at the recent viewers and contacts them, to see if one of them may offer more than the current offeree, or at least leaves a message that if he does not hear back within 24 hours he will assume they are not interested.

Many Agents receive an offer, nobody else has contacted them with an offer, so why confuse the issue, get it sold to that offeror as quickly as possible and with the least effort. Whereas The Real Estate Agent rings around those people who have recently viewed and maybe just haven't got around to contacting you yet. Many instances of this spring to mind but within the last week of this being written, a property at an asking price of 'offers in the region of £89,000' and upon receipt of an offer of £82,000, a viewer was rung 'who had not had time to ring' even though they had viewed 10 days beforehand. A bidding situation was entered into and a sale price of £93,000 realised. That's when you should ring the viewers for feedback.

COMMUNICATION

To take the feedback situation further, I often hear Estate Agents being criticised for lack of communication. 'We put our property on the market and have heard absolutely nothing'. I am sure many of you reading this book will have had that experience. In an ideal world, of course, you would get contact. The truth is that with current fee levels, lack of turnover and the increased number of properties Agents have on their books, and for a variety of reasons, it has become far more difficult to keep in touch with the most important person, the Agent's client. Contacting vendors to tell them nothing is happening is not only one of the least pleasant aspects of the sales negotiators' jobs, but also from the Agents point of view, the least productive. Again, as with feedback, the negotiators' efforts are better directed to looking to their contacts to see if he can interest someone in the property, or to properties where offers are being received and there is more activity. If the fees were higher, then of course the Real Estate Agent would be able to improve communication. It is impossible to employ enough people to do the communication and feedback to the expectations of the public/client and run a business that is profitable, particularly if you are not selling financial services and only getting sellers' fees from each sale. The Real Estate Agent recognises this and also recognises the dangers of it. On leaving the client, prior to instructions, he always says 'please feel able to contact us if you are worried about anything, wondering what's going on, then please feel able to ring us. If you have not heard from us it is because we don't have anything to discuss, or feel you have to know. If you are passing the office pop in, because we do try and do courtesy calls where there is little action and if you have been in, we know you are up to date and OK'. As a Vendor you should remember that communication is a two-way thing and I have to say that where people say to me that 'we never heard anything from the Agent' I usually pose the question, then why didn't you ring them. Get the mobile telephone number of the person who valued it and if you are dissatisfied, ring him or her.

It should also be remembered that you should be working as a team with your Agent. It should not be a 'them and us' situation. You should be seeking to help them, so that if you think of something, if you know something about a purchaser, contact them, speak to them, don't be frightened to ask questions on how things are going, or if you want to know about a particular person you think is interested, inform them. If your circumstances have changed, e.g. you have suddenly seen a house that you really want and you could afford, even at a slightly lower price being realised for your own property, then communicate it. There is an obvious assumption by a client that when he does not hear from his Agent, the Agent is doing nothing. In the Real Estate Agent's case, nothing could be further from the truth. Agents get paid by success only, not on the work they do and particularly in difficult times, and a slow market, the Real Estate Agent is looking for every opportunity to sell a property. He will have regular meetings with his sales staff and will look at or call out the name of each property on the list they have to sell. He will be told if there were any viewings, if they have decided to take advantage of newspaper features, such as 'Property of the Week' and place that property in it. He will be looking at the decision as to whether to advertise that property, whether there should be a change in slant on the advertising, particularly on Rightmove, to make people stop and look at the property again. He will be asking the question whether a change of price is appropriate and likely to increase the number of viewings. The Real Estate Agent will be asking these questions on a regular basis, he just does not have the time to communicate everything that is going on within the office as he would like to. Only when the answer is yes to one of the proposals, does he communicate them to you and give you his suggested way forward. He will then take your instructions. For the best results you will be working as a team, putting your heads together and making decisions, but always remember that The Real Estate Agent should be advising you and then doing as he is told (taking your instructions), having pointed out the pros and cons of each proposed way forward.

OFFERS

The property is marketed, viewings have taken place; interest is being shown. The house is attracting immediate interest and the office is busy arranging viewings, because The Real Estate Agent has priced it correctly rather than setting a high price and consequentially nobody asking to see it. I believe that in most Estate Agents offices, very little training is given as to how to handle offers. The reason is simple, some ridiculous idea that the Agent asks the client what to do. You, as the client ask for valuation expertise, you ask to be told about marketing and you chose an Estate Agent, yet at this point, the majority of modern Estate Agents will ring you with an offer then ask you what you think they should do. This is one of the main pieces of expertise you are paying for. People used to move house every seven years in the '80s, and just before the credit crunch it was every seventeen years, and in 2014 it was every 23 years. These days you don't do it very often, so you don't get a lot of practice. The Agent should be advising you as to the options regarding the offer, advising you how he thinks they should proceed and then taking your instructions, not just asking you what you want to do.

On Monday morning after a weekend of viewings, the first offer is received. The asking price is £110,000 and the first offer from Buyer A is £95,000. As per the Estate Agents Act, the offer is put in writing to the Vendor and as per the modern Code of Practice, a letter is sent to the Purchaser, telling them that their offer has been put forward. The law states that the offer has to be qualified. In other words, the questions have to be asked:

1. Do you have a house to sell before you can buy?

2. Do you have a mortgage arranged, or is cash immediately available?

When instructing your Agent, you should ask the question whether or not they will put offers forward with the questions being asked, or do they not deem the purchaser to be qualified until they have seen their Financial Adviser, where they have one.

Basically the qualification process was made law and the corporate agents used it as an excuse to not to put the offer forward, unless and until the prospective purchaser had seen their Qualifier. Low and behold, their Qualifier just happens to be a fully paid up Mortgage Adviser. How convenient. The law was actually put in place for the corporate good and to allow the 'one-stop-shop' conflict of interest idea to prosper. The Real Estate Agent will ask the questions, but it will not be necessary to place the person before a Mortgage Adviser, which can take a considerable period of time. The letter you will receive from The Real Estate Agent will say either:

1. The prospective purchaser does/ does not have a property to sell and we may or will not be instructed in the sale or

2. The prospective purchaser has a mortgage arranged and we are making enquiries to substantiate this.

This can be done by a quick phone call to a Mortgage Adviser, or in some cases a Certificate of Mortgage given by a Bank or Building Society. It is not necessary to haul the prospective purchaser before some Mortgage Adviser who then has to go through the whole rigmarole of compliance procedures. Of course, the idea is to see what mortgage they have arranged and see if they can better it, to sell their product and by the way, do you need life insurance as well?

The Real Estate Agent has sent the letter to Person A, he doesn't have a house to sell and he has a mortgage and is ready to proceed.

Whenever new members of staff arrive at an Estate Agents Office, it is one of the most difficult things to do, to stop them ringing the client as soon as they have an offer without having given any thought to what advice they should be giving regarding that offer. The Real Estate Agent does a number of things upon receipt of that offer to put himself into a position so that when he rings the client he is able to advise him:

A) Check the Viewing Sheets to see if other people have viewed recently, ring them and tell them that there is an offer and see if they would be interested in the property at a higher level.

B) There is an interest there and it is worth waiting a day or two for them to formulate their finances etc.

C) Decide whether or not the offer is within the valuation guideline, but at this early stage, keep an open mind.

The advice to the client is: Mr Client, we have received an offer of £95,000, we have checked with 6 other viewers and 4 are interested. Further, we have 3 more viewings within the next 4 days, so given the level of interest we think we should not accept this offer at this stage. There is, of course, a risk here. The alternative and easier route for the Agent is to suggest we throw it back to him at £100,000 and see what he says, or simply ask 'What are you willing to accept'? This type of Agent is the Quick Deal Agent. He is not the maximising price Agent. He is not The Real Estate Agent. Again, there is no absolute right or wrong. Is it wrong to offer the price back at £100,000 and get it without involving other people? Of course it is not as long as the client has been fully informed of the other potential people and the other offers that could come. It may be that by getting a quick sale, he then secures the house he needs. All the circumstances have to be taken into account and in reaching the advice to the client, the Real Estate Agent looks at his valuation and takes a view on if he waits, is he likely to get more than the current offer. Let's assume that we believe from enquiry of the viewers, that other offers will be received.

It should also be remembered that if a mortgage is likely to be arranged through the selling Agency, then the mortgage broker Agent may in some cases show favour for this purchaser, rather than others following.

Purchaser B, having been rung and told of the offer of £95,000 then rings in and offers £97,000. Purchaser B is cash; he is a 'Buy to Let' man and has just sold a property and the money is in the Bank. A quick call to his Solicitor can confirm this, the appropriate letters go out. The purchaser does not have a house to sell and therefore we will not be involved in getting instructions on his property and a mortgage is not required as it is cash.

Person C rings in and they are prepared to offer more, but they have a house to sell. Does The Real Estate Agent discount this, is it worth looking at since they have a house to sell? Again it depends upon the circumstances, but the Real Estate Agent is negotiating here and he is trying to build a price, he is trying to build a situation. This is proper negotiation, using the demand for the property to maximise it. The Real Estate Agent will ask to value the property that the individual has to sell. He will give them the valuation, with a base figure on which to calculate their best and final offer. If they are working off the base figure that he gives them, he knows that their offer will eventually come to fruition, once their house has sold. Person C offers £105,000, but subject to his house sale which has been valued. Purchasers A & B, now know that there is somebody willing to pay far more than they are, although it is subject to sale. Already their sights are being increased given there is an offer of £105,000 and they have only offered £95,000 & £97,000 respectively. The letter, compliant with the Estate Agency Act goes out and states the offer of £105,000 is subject to a house sale. We may be instructed in the sale, the purchaser will require a mortgage which we understand is to be arranged, a telephone call requesting that they take mortgage advice immediately, to put them in as strong a position as possible, is given to Purchaser C. At this point the vendor is contacted. The suggestion is we believe both the mortgage and the cash purchaser should be treated equally; they are both as likely to be able to purchase. We have assumed that the property is in reasonable condition and the mortgage is unlikely to fail because of survey (and other considerations). We are advising the client that we ask Purchaser C for a best and final offer, so that:

1) The client knows how far he is prepared to go and Purchaser C feels he has had a chance.

2) A higher offer may well give more confidence to Purchasers A & B and make them feel that the property is worth nearer the asking price.

Purchaser D rings in, he has a house to sell but this house is in the best area of town and will sell like hot cakes at the right level. He is prepared to give a best offer of the full asking price of £110,000 subject to the sale of his house. Again the offer letters go out, the valuation must be arranged. If he can work off the base figure given by the valuer then whilst selling to him may take a little longer, The Real Estate Agent has the courage of his convictions and his ability to value, and if there is a big price differential and if it fits in with what the Vendor is trying to achieve, it may be worth waiting for Purchaser

D to sell his house. In the meantime, Purchasers A & B are bidding, but at £100,000 Purchaser A drops out and we are left with Purchaser B offering £100,000 cash on a Buy to Let basis. Purchaser C is asked for a best offer, which is £108,000 and Purchaser D has already offered £110,000 best and final.

The client is then asked what is most important, the highest amount or the speed of sale. The normal situation is that the property is offered back to Purchaser B (the cash and buy to let man) at a price: usually slightly discounted from the more complicated offers. For our exercise and purposes, we will say it is offered back at £108,000, the Buy to Let man offers £106,000, there is a little to-ing and fro-ing and a deal is agreed at £107,000 with Purchaser B, in the full knowledge of what all the interested parties were prepared to offer.

Unless your Agent is researching the parties, going through the offers situation in such a manner, they are not doing their job properly. Selling and agreeing a price to the first offeree without consulting other people who have viewed may get a quick sale, but it is lazy estate agency. You cannot be sure you have maximised the price, if you are not given the opportunity and although the Real Estate Agent may charge you a higher fee, he will more than make it for you, most particularly at the point of negotiation.

The question the Real Estate Agent asks himself, before accepting any offer is, 'on the evidence of our marketing, general interest in the property and on the comparable evidence of our valuation, if this offer is not accepted, do

I think I will get a lot more by waiting?' He then advises the client, they look at the situation and the reason for sale together, then the vendor gives his instructions.

From the above, you will understand that dealing with all these would-be purchasers is far more difficult than one might first imagine and really a considerable skill. You are building a price, building confidence and using the level of interest to do so. This happens, because you have priced it at a level which is within the property's general affordability. The modern way with many Agents is to overprice and the effect is that you do not get this type of competition. Some people, after a period of time, view the property, expecting to get it for far less. Indeed, most Agents no longer expect to sell a property quickly, because they know that they have put it on at such a high level. It is almost as though a property is expected to sit on the market for a long period of time and then sell eventually, for a lot less money. If Agents do get interest, then rather than take offer and counter offer, they merely ask for a best and final offer. This can work, but my experience is that unless you build a price first, you start from too low a platform. Strangely, the British public are asked for their best offer, but often they don't give it to you. They give what they hope and think they might get it for. Then when told the property has been sold elsewhere they give a further offer.

There is no course that you can go on to learn negotiation. The Real Estate Agent recognises that it is something his staff has to learn but it can only be learnt by experience. It is about making a deal come together and getting people to offer more. If you think they can afford to offer more, you then have to put the argument forward as to why they should do so. It is a thin line between being overly intrusive and, putting ideas into peoples' heads as to why they should make this happen and not lose the opportunity of buying a house which will improve their lifestyle and quality of life. That is what the Real Estate Agent is selling and he measures every word of a conversation to bring the deal together, for everybody's interests. How do I know this to be true, because of the number of times I have taken over a floundering negotiation and been able to pull it together. It is about experience and authority and very simply, the more experience and empathy a negotiator has the more likely he is to be able to pull things together. Very simply, there is no substitute for knowledge and experience and negotiation is not just about asking the Vendor whether he is prepared to accept the offer.

TAKING THE PROPERTY OFF THE MARKET

Let's assume that in the case above, Purchasers B & C will bid no further and at £110,000, the Vendor decides to sell to Person D. The Vendor is not buying another property, it was bequeathed to him. The extra money is far more than he will get in interest from having the sale proceed quickly and putting the sale money in a savings account in a Bank. The Real Estate Agent is confident that the purchaser's property will sell quickly, because of the area it is in and because the price that Purchaser D is working off, is within the Real Estate Agents valuation band for his property. Under the Ombudsman's Code of Practice, if a property is not to be taken off the market but still offered for sale, the prospective purchaser has to be told. Some Estate Agents, especially corporate, will advise the client of the hard line of keeping the property on the market, so that other interested parties may come along. In effect, they are merely agreeing a price in principle, even when they sell to a cash buyer. Indeed, they may, but generally speaking, the Real Estate Agent has marketed the property at the right level; the depth of market in terms of value has been found by the initial marketing exercise that he has done and it is unlikely that someone will come out of the woodwork and pay very much more than the £110,000 already offered. The Real Estate Agent has to decide whether to advise his client to take the property off the market or not. He will advise his client to do so if the purchaser is working off his valuation on the sale of his own house, and if Purchaser D's house is considered as saleable or more saleable at that level as the Vendor's property.

It should be remembered that this is a human situation and human nature will come through, whatever. If you leave a property on the market, two things may happen:

1) The prospective purchaser thinks he may not get it and he therefore continues to look elsewhere. His commitment is not as great. The result of this is when the prospective purchaser does receive an offer on his home, he is perhaps not prepared to accept a lower figure on his own house to secure the subject property, because his commitment is not as great, or he may well find another property.

2) To guard against the disappointment of possibly not getting the property, he actually starts thinking of reasons why he doesn't want it. This is human nature and it happens to whoever is in this position, because they can't help it. It particularly happens where the purchaser in the initial throes of trying to get the property, has over-committed, or perhaps where the property needs a lot of initial structural improvements or modernisation.

Thus, not taking a property off the market can work against the Vendor in a manner that is not often perceived. If you take a property off the market and say give the purchaser a selling period of 4 – 6 weeks to sell his own after which the situation will be re-assessed, then the prospective purchaser commits in every way, shape and form. He does not look elsewhere, is positive about the work that needs to be done, and when a slightly lower offer comes in on his own than required, then he will still make every effort to make the situation work, and purchase because he is still fully committed.

Therefore, The Real Estate Agent will advise clients to take the property off the market in most situations and in the above situation, has even taken it off the market when there is a property to sell. He is confident in his valuation and therefore felt able to recommend this, as he deals in what will happen, not what might happen, because he values correctly and places a proper asking price on the property, which will create interest.

THE QUIET TIME

After the excitement of viewings and the acceptance of the offer, there is a quiet period. During this period the Vendors Solicitors are sending out contracts and the Purchasers Solicitors are making enquiries. The mortgage has been applied for by the mortgage broker or if the purchaser is dealing with a Bank, the purchaser's solicitor will be in contact with them and it is much easier if the purchaser's solicitor can act for both the purchaser and the purchaser's bank, in preparing the mortgage deed, etc. As the mortgage is being processed, the quiet time abruptly comes to an end, with the valuation/survey for the mortgage company. The Real Estate Agent will always try and make sure that the arrangement is made through his office. This means The Real Estate Agent knows who the surveyor and his company is and can get hold of him if it is necessary.

THE PURCHASERS SURVEYOR/VALUATION

You should expect your Estate Agent to have a good understanding of structure, and a professional method of valuation. This is the time when perhaps it can be most necessary. There is a presumption and indeed a rightful expectation that all Surveyors and Valuers know what they are doing. Most certainly to carry out a mortgage valuation, they will need to be members of the Royal Institution of Chartered Surveyors. Let's make a presumption that the valuation being carried out is on a mid-terraced Victorian dwelling house. This means that a mortgage valuation will be carried out for the Building Society in terms of whether the property is a proper security for the money being lent, and will not necessarily have the name of the surveyor or company on it. The purchaser will be given a copy of this but it will not have the name of the surveyors on it. However, if he opts for the Home Buyer Report (this is a private more detailed report on structure, at extra cost) done by the Valuation Surveyor, his name should be available to him on the Home Buyer Report.

The vast majority of mortgage valuations are now carried out by corporate surveyors either directly or indirectly employed by the Banks themselves. Whereas local Valuers used to value, these surveyors sometimes cover great distances to carry out valuations. They therefore simply do not have the local knowledge on valuation, so in this first instance, it is not appropriate to assume they really do know what they are doing. Were they to value the property without being told the sale price, they probably would be miles out. Further, as they are largely employed by the Bank lending the money, their concern is not that the correct price is being paid, but that the Bank's money is secure. As long as it is then they may well value at the sale price, so that the deal goes through. Hardly the independent valuation that the purchaser thought he was getting. The modern Home Buyer Report reflects the importance of the need to do something in terms of the colours green, amber and red. Therefore, there is little chance of getting two Surveyors to totally agree on the importance of certain items.

It is quite likely that different surveyors will have different opinions. Whilst an older surveyor may say in a Victorian terraced house, 'the sub-floor ventilation is not up to modern standards but has stood the test of time', the more modern surveyor will say 'the sub-floor ventilation does not reach modern standards and is inadequate', and that steps should be taken to improve it. This completely ignores the fact that the timber used in Victorian times was far better seasoned and often pitch pine in floors, thus withstanding moisture attack far better.

Structural problems to a purchaser in the written word can look absolutely dire and completely put them off. What should be a joyful and exciting purchase suddenly looks as though you are buying a heap of rubble. With the greatest respect to many people practicing Estate Agency they have little chance of pulling this round, nor are they in a position to re-negotiate the price properly, as they do not know whether all the remarks are completely justified and the cost implications are correct therefore, because they know very little about structural problems.

When things are straightforward an Agent with little knowledge gets away with it, but when things go wrong, a Real Estate Agent with knowledge of structure and property law, is more likely to win the day.

When an adverse report has been given, and in that case almost certainly a down valuation, the Real Estate Agent will ask for a copy of the report. If the purchaser is truly interested he will give you one and the point is made by the Real Estate Agent, 'unless we know what is being said how can we possibly agree to a reduction'? With the report in hand, the Real Estate Agent will inspect the property as a Surveyor and look at the issues. It is then his advice that some of these issues are real and are likely to come up again, should the property be re-marketed and re-sold. There is, of course, the issue as to whether he took some of these into account in the first place in his valuation. The Real Estate Agent will speak to the vendor and establish what he believes are fair points of the survey and that the purchaser will have to address in real terms. There is then the issue of cost and whether all of this cost should be borne by the vendor and indeed by how much the vendor can reduce. Having agreed with the vendor that certain things will need to be done in the short term and these will be fully compensated for, whilst less urgent longer term things can only partially be compensated for. The vendor gives the Real Estate Agent a lien to drop so far. It is then up to his negotiation skills with the purchaser, to get the best deal he can for the vendor again, where affordability is the key. The next step obviously is contacting the purchaser, but it is also a re-building of confidence. A Surveyor has to cover himself and it is a simple fact that the written word often looks far worse than the reality. The attempt has to be made to re-build confidence in the property and to realistically assess what has to be done with the purchaser. The Real Estate Agent, being a Surveyor, may well inspect the property with the purchasers, report in hand. On this basis, more often than not, with everything so close, there is a real will to make the whole thing work; the Real Estate Agent, with that extra confidence of property knowledge and understanding of property and structure, will do this far more effectively than those who have no structural knowledge at all.

The fact that modern Building Society Valuers rarely try and value or actually down value, is of assistance to the Vendors. With few high loan to value ratio mortgages offered by the lenders, the Building Society Surveyor usually puts the value as the Sale Price, as long as they feel the loan is adequately secured, but retentions are put on for work required.

After all, the important thing to the lender (who often employs the surveyor through a sister company) is that they get the business, never mind the purchaser may be interested to know he is paying above the real depth of market value.

However, sometimes at this stage, a renegotiation of the purchase price has to be made. It may be that the purchaser simply cannot afford the price that he offered, because of the extra works he has found need to be done.

It may be that the property was down valued to an extent that he simply needs to reduce his offer as that has affected what he can afford. However, we will assume that these re-negotiations either are not necessary, or take place successfully. Your cash/mortgage purchase is possible and you wish to proceed at the full price agreed, or the new price agreed. It is now up to the Solicitors.

THE SOLICITOR STAGE

Increasingly, Solicitors do not carry out any work that causes the vendor or purchaser to build up a bill, until the mortgage offer is out, or until there is absolutely no doubt that the purchaser intends to proceed. The reason for this is that if they spend time doing the work, they incur charges and if the whole thing is aborted, they have great difficulty recovering their fees. There is also the valid point that in the vast majority of cases, they do not wish to incur the client unnecessary costs. However, this means that work which could have been done simultaneously, is not done and so you can anticipate that it is now a fact that completion times, from agreement of the sale to completion, have extended from 2 ½ to 3 ½ months and even 4 months.

Where there is absolutely no chain, it is a cash purchase it should really take no longer than two months from agreement of the sale to completion. Where chains are involved, there are other people and other factors. However, it is a simple fact that many Solicitors do not have a clue what is going on up the chain, when everybody else is hoping to complete. In many cases, the Solicitors have no idea the identity of who is at the bottom of the chain, or no idea where it ends at the top. The Real Estate Agent has already researched this information and all this has been taken into account, when you agreed the sale/purchase. It makes sense, therefore, for this information to be provided to the Solicitor. The Real Estate Agent sets out this information so that the Solicitors know who else is involved, how long the chain is and can e-mail other solicitors involved in the chain, with non-legal situations, the practicalities of completion dates, waiting for mortgage offers, etc. Wherever possible, it makes sense to have an Exchange of Contracts with a completion 2 - 4 weeks later. Increasingly, exchange and completion takes place on the same day.

CHASING THE CHAIN

Purchaser D's house is now on the market and an offer is received from a party who has accepted an offer on their own house, who in turn has sold to someone who has sold to a First-time-buyer. This is the much maligned chain situation, but the chain situation is totally necessary in the English system, as most people who are buying have a house to sell, and only by managing them properly can you get volumes of people moved. The offer letters go out, pointing out that this buyer has a house to sell, the Real Estate Agent will not be instructed in the sale, a mortgage is required but The Real Estate Agent will not be arranging it. It will point out that the purchaser has Sold Subject to Contract. It is, of course, The Real Estate Agent's duty to get as high a price as possible for Purchaser D's house and a sale price is negotiated, in excess of the base figure and an offer is accepted, subject to the agreed sales and the small viable chain, completed by the first time buyer, who makes all the moves possible. The vendor of the original house has been informed. Before this happens however, the Real Estate Agent has been busy speaking to parties involved in the chain - it is all an assessment of risk. It is a constant amazement to me that when you ring Estate Agents who have accepted an offer from someone in a chain, that they have not checked out the exact position of the person below them. Have you spoken to the purchaser's solicitors to confirm this? No.

The Real Estate Agent will speak to the solicitors of the purchaser buying Purchaser D's property and find out who they have sold to and what their position is. He will also find out the contact details of the solicitors to that purchaser and confirm the situation with them. He will then speak to the next purchaser's solicitor and confirm the situation with them and find out if it is a first time buyer who has a mortgage and is able to proceed. He is then able to advise his client that the chain may reasonably be relied upon. Some Solicitors will refuse to discuss their clients' position, and it may be necessary or actually better to speak to the Agents involved; at the end of the day, the Real Estate Agent is not desirous of detailed financial information, just an understanding of the persons' ability to proceed. Enquiries should be made of the position regarding surveys. If surveys have not been carried out, enquiries should be made as to the age of the houses involved and the likelihood of there being a problem with survey. On assessment of all this, it is then a case of saying to both clients, that there is a completed chain upon which you may reasonably rely on completing. The longer the chain and the more people there are involved, the greater the likelihood of difficulties.

The Real Estate Agents work does not stop there. If you have a chain he has to keep on top of it. He may have a fellow agent who is equally thorough, but the chances are he will not. It is amazing how many times chains have fallen through at the bottom because, for example, a property near the bottom of the chain was down valued, and nobody tried to work with the parties, to make sure it happens with all parties reducing to make up the shortfall, or worse, the solicitors further up the chain, don't even know the chain is in jeopardy. The last thing an Agent wants is for it to fall through at the last minute and yet it is amazing how many modern Estate Agents wash their hands of the deal once they have agreed terms, and thereby lose their chance of a commission which would have come to them, with a little extra effort and thought.

The Real Estate Agent has already chased the chain, to list all the parties involved, who is buying from whom, list their Solicitors and the latter's e-mail addresses. This means the Solicitors can easily let each other know of progress, completion dates, etc. In some cases, chains have collapsed and no-one knows, because the Solicitor acting for the person giving backword had not informed the solicitor that his client was no longer proceeding, even though there is a normal requirement to immediately return the legal papers. Sometimes there can be a solicitor in a chain who is not communicating and does not appear to be progressing legal work. The client to the solicitor can be contacted through the Estate Agency contact and told to check with his solicitor as to how things are going, as other people want to complete. As soon as possible, it is essential to try and work to a date and it is so much better to exchange and then complete say 2/4 weeks later so that everybody knows what's going on and can arrange removals. Yet in many cases, the modern way appears to be to exchange and complete on one day, which can create mayhem as often happens, the mortgage company does not get the money through in time, or some paperwork is not ready for one of the transactions, and people are sat with removal vans outside the property, unable to complete because something is not in place.

However, we will assume completion takes place.

THE REAL ESTATE AGENTS INVOICE

It is customary for the invoice to be sent to the Solicitor. The Solicitor then seeks approval to pay out of the arranged monies. An Advice Note (which does not attract VAT) is usually sent early to the Solicitor so that he knows what monies will be required on completion. He should check for any extras, that it complies with the contract and then on completion, the solicitor will normally pay the Agents from the sale proceeds, but must always seek the Vendors approval first.

The Real Estate Agent will hope that you feel that his fee was well earned. He will hope, that because of his advice, you perhaps made more money than you would have done on the property, that he has helped you with any purchase and he has also helped you through the legal stages and the move allows you to get on with your life. The Real Estate Agent is proactive and it is about making things happen. It is not only about understanding property, but understanding people and their needs for reassurance, or not. Different clients require care of a different type, simply because of their personalities. He will not see this just as a job paid for, but he will hope that if he moved you locally then in the future you would look to him again, because you were satisfied. To The Real Estate Agent, it is not just about money, but it is also about providing a caring service to move people at different stages of their lives, and getting job satisfaction.

SECTION II – BUYING A HOUSE

Chapter 5

To Buy or Sell First

The Real Estate Agent thinks of his job as moving people. The vast majority of people who purchase a house, have a house to sell and the real art of agency is not selling one house at a time, but building a chain and making 4 or 5 sales, starting with a big house and finishing with a First Time Buyer's house. In the '70s and '80s building chains was commonplace, but then came over valuation. A Real Estate Agent could build a chain of 2 or 3 alright, but other Agents would tell the fourth person in the chain that their house was worth £40,000 more than it really was, to get the house to sell at too high an asking price, and of course the chain did not happen. It takes time for that fourth person to realise that their house isn't going to achieve what they were told it was going to achieve, by the over valuing agent, and the three people in the chain would not wait that long. As chains no longer worked as easily, coming backwards, the effect of 'Free Valuations' and consumerism took hold; Vendors began to get lots of Agents to value their house. Quite right I hear you say. The problem is that some large Corporate Agents involved at the time, came up with the bright idea of telling people to sell their house first. Some are prepared to do it, but the majority are not.

This is a much easier concept. The agent does not have to rely on his valuations as the chains build from the bottom and the person coming to you has already sold and knows what they have got and what they have to spend. The problem with that is that you are asking people to sell their house, not knowing where they are going to go, how much they are going to have to pay, and how long it is going to be before they find the house that they want. In other words, you are introducing massive uncertainty and people do not like uncertainty. Hence, all of a sudden, instead of moving house, as it were from house to house and knowing where you are going, it suddenly becomes a situation where having sold, you have to frantically find a house, and of course you did not always find the house that you wanted or if you did, you couldn't afford it. The only option was to rent, which most people did not want to do. The result of that was that people extended their existing house instead of selling it. If you went onto a housing estate, instead of Estate Agents Boards and moving people to larger houses, it was builders' boards with people extending. The big Estate Agents chains, through their lack of expertise, had introduced the first whammy. Banks and Building Societies anxious to get the business had reduced their core business, the mortgage business available, because very simply, people stopped moving. The move had been made so difficult and uncertain that they simply stayed put or preferred to extend. (See Chapter on Transaction Levels).

If you are a First Time Buyer, if you are buying a second/holiday home, and if you have enough money that you can purchase without the sale of your own home, or if you can get a bridging loan then you do not have a problem, you can buy first. You can place an offer that is not dependent upon another sale and the Agent you are trying to purchase from, knows it is viable and not sale dependent. If you are dealing with The Real Estate Agent and you are bridging, it is still possible that he may prefer another offeree who has the money and does not need to bridge, as many bridgers ultimately don't do it, or then sell their existing property and run the sale in with the completion of that property and the complexity of other sales linked in, etc.

In the main, the vast majority of people who wish to move home, have a house to sell and are faced with that dear old 'chicken and egg' situation. Do you sell first, go into rented and then look, or do you look, find a property and then sell your own. The fact is, there is absolutely no right and wrong in this, but there are disadvantages and advantages of each way forward, and there are circumstances, for example if you are moving out of the area, or if you are looking for a retirement bungalow, which possibly in terms of practicability, tip the balance in favour one way or the other.

It should be remembered that a house is a vehicle for your life and it is you and your peace of mind that is most important. People deal with situations very differently and people handle uncertainty very differently. If being in rented accommodation and not owning a house and the emotional instability which that can give you will not suit you, then don't do it. If it is the case, that by looking at a number of properties before selling your own and losing them because you have not sold your own, you are going to get emotionally attached to one and totally disappointed if you don't get it, then don't do it. I have, however, become a great believer in fate in the sense that I have seen people lose properties that they desperately wanted and be terribly disappointed, only to find another property and be grateful that they never got the first one. Whilst I believe that the human mind has an amazing ability to adjust and make the most out of a situation, things simply can work out for the best.

Chapter 6

Selling First

The biggest disadvantage is that you can be in rented accommodation for years and not be settled. The biggest advantage of selling first is that it puts you in a strong position and you are not sale-dependent when offering on another property. However, the advantage is not quite as great as people imagine, since others are doing it. So often a prospective purchase will say 'I am sold and in rented accommodation' expecting this to be a major advantage when all the people offering are in the same position. When a new property comes onto the market in a reasonable area, properly priced, there are actually other people in the same situation, but at least you have the option to pay the most and secure it. Where properties have been over priced and are on the market for a long time, then obviously you can proceed and are in a position to do so, if you can negotiate that price down.

However, many people are simply not prepared to sell their house first, as they do not want to be out of house and home, not knowing where they are going and how much they are going to have to pay. In other words, you have accepted an offer on your existing property, not knowing whether that will give you enough money to buy another. Obviously, personal circumstances affect this, but if you are at the margin of your affordability then it can be an issue. You sell a house for a price and then find you cannot afford to buy the type of house you want to replace the one you had and this is the principal risk involved.

If you sold your house and were in rented accommodation in June 2002, you lost 20% in terms of your affordability. In other words, in 2002 prices generally rose approximately 30% and it was in the middle of the year that something happened with Bank lending that made everyone's affordability that much greater. If you were in rented accommodation at that time, you lost ground. You sold your house for 20% less than you could have got a few weeks later, and you had to pay 20% more for the house you purchased. The advantage of being in the market, i.e. owning a house, is if the house you are trying to buy is going up, so is the one you are trying to sell.

The Real Estate Agent understands that it is the differential between prices that is important. If prices are going up the vendor gets more, but pays more. If you are out of the market i.e. in rented accommodation, there is a danger if prices are going up, but it can be a good thing if prices are coming down. If you are moving house from a good and very much sought after locality, if your house is priced correctly when you sell first, it will sell within a short period of time. I think there are real reasons for selling your house first if you are moving out of the area for example with a job move. Apart from anything else, if you have a family, you all move together, but if you move to an area where there is a lot of property on the market, an area possibly not quite as sought after as where you are leaving, then with lots of property available, having sold your own at a reasonable price, you can get a 'good deal' on one of the many properties that are available in your new location. This is particularly so since the credit crunch and the subsequent huge drop in transaction levels, as demand in some areas has held up, and in others, there are very few sales.

One of the most disadvantaged type of people are the elderly, trying to buy a bungalow or retirement flat, usually within easy level walking distance of shops or on a bus route. For this type of property, invariably there are enough prospective purchasers who have built up enough money to buy without selling and if an elderly couple are not ready to proceed unfortunately they will be disappointed a number of times, as cash comes out of the woodwork for the type of property they are looking for. For this group of people, the leap in the dark is probably the hardest and if they are downsizing to that type of property, they have the greatest need to do it.

One of the practical disadvantages of selling your house first is that you end up with two sets of removal costs and will obviously pay money in rent. Usually if you are renting, the minimum rental period is six months and therefore if you find a house in the short term, you may have two or three months extra rent to pay.

Whilst the biggest disadvantage of selling your house first, is the uncertainty, there is another. Unless you have seen a property, unless you link your sale to a purchase, you do not know what you could have accepted. The aim is to move you so that you can get on with your life. Let's say you are moving from Lancashire to Yorkshire (a defection but we will allow it!) and you are asking £110,000 for your property. You haven't a clue what you can buy, so how do you know what you can accept. It may be that you are trying to hold out and sell for a price that actually is more than you need. You may lose offers at a proper level, because you have been told that your house is worth more, (remember if you sell well, you sell early), lose these offers and then find that you did not need as much as you thought when you actually buy. The big advantage though, whilst that is a danger of course, if all goes swimmingly, is you get the figure that you feel is reasonably achievable and proper on your own property, you go into rented in Yorkshire, you know what you can afford, you are ready to proceed, you find a house and you buy it.

Chapter 7

Buying First

However, where a move is not enforced as the above and is perhaps because their children are getting older, and would move locally, then more people will not sell first. Therefore, for a more active market and to get people moving, the Real Estate Agent encourages looking before they sell.

I am amazed that Estate Agencies tell people not to look until they have sold. On the basis that most people who are trying to move have a house to sell, this means that everybody goes home, puts their house on the market and nobody looks. Are they for real? The Real Estate Agent will encourage you to look, not only for your own good, but also for the good of his own business. He knows that 'once a purchaser has seen a property, it stops being just about money, but about being a home'. This means that if you get a perceived low offer on your own property, then you are more likely to accept it, if you can buy a house that you have already seen and at a differential you can afford. If you get less, you pay less, it is the differential that counts and unless you are in a position to offer on properties that you have seen, you do not know whether that 'low offer' on your own property will be enough to move you. You do not know what you can afford to accept! By linking together in this fashion, the Real Estate Agent gets you moved and improves his own business.

The only disadvantage with looking before you have sold is that you get disappointed as emotionally you get involved with hoping to get a property and then lose it because you have not been able to sell your own. However, what is worse, is not knowing where you are going, having sold your own property. I have devoted a whole chapter to Transaction Levels but unless Estate Agents get people moving from house to house to house and not via rented accommodation, transaction levels will never fully recover. It is not only economic circumstances that make the buoyancy of a market, AGENTS MAKE MARKETS.

Let us assume you have seen a lot of properties that you like because as we speak, there are lots on the market. There is nothing wrong in agreeing a price in principle, subject to the sale of your own. It may even be that The Real Estate Agent thinks a property that you are interested in is not as saleable as your own. For example, property outside of town is not selling as well as property in town. Therefore, as long as he prices yours correctly, your town house will sell far more easily than the property in the country. You have been realistic with the sale price and he may be prepared to advise the country property owner to take his off the market to you on the basis of the valuation on your own house and the fact that your property is more saleable. You won't know, unless you get involved. Unless The Real Estate Agent involves you, he won't know either.

Some Agents today seem reluctant to even take an offer from a prospective purchaser because they do not have a sale. Why not agree a price in principle and give the prospective offeree something definite to aim for?

Let's assume that you have looked at a number of properties and you have found three. You may offer in principle subject to the sale of your own, and see what the various purchasers are thinking, or you may place your house on the market at a realistic level, see what offers occur and then, knowing your differential of affordability, place an offer on one or even each of these houses. In the example above, say you put your property on the market at £110,000, you are expecting £100,000, and you can afford to offer £150,000 for your next larger home. You get offered a maximum of £90,000 on your own property, you can therefore only offer £140,000 but you don't know whether or not such an offer on one of those properties will be acceptable. Remember it is the differential that is important. Unless you have seen something and unless you have offered, you actually don't know whether you can accept £90,000 as opposed to the £100,000 you thought you needed to get in order to move on with your life. So, on the assumption that your buyer cannot afford any more, hold on to his offer of £90,000 and say you are trying to purchase a property on that basis. That is Real Estate Agency advice, that is linking sales, that is making things happen and it is much more necessary and required in a market where prices are dropping, than the easy market, where prices are rising.

Those Agents who actually discourage you from looking until you have sold your house or unless you have your house on the market, saying you are not a serious purchaser, are plain wrong. Of course you are a serious purchaser; you just don't want to move without having found somewhere; to know where you are going. Thus, by encouraging people in the right way, The Real Estate Agent will make the market happen and will get you into a position whereby possibly you can move, albeit accepting a slightly lower price than you had hoped to achieve. The refusal to allow you to view if your house is not on the market can also be a cynical attempt by the Agent to get your house to sell. In many cases, that Agent will put people off moving altogether as they won't be totally committed to move until they have seen a house they like.

In a local market, where people are moving within the area, The Real Estate Agent welcomes people with houses to sell. If everybody is told to go home and put their houses on the market and not look, nobody looks. If people look, they get enthused and become more proactive, perhaps reducing their price, or spending more on advertising to find a buyer to try and sell their own. If that house sells to somebody who has a house to sell, or the Agent has two houses on the market, it means there is a greater likelihood of one of them selling, and the upward chain being put together. Many modern Estate Agents do not understand this; all they understand is selling one house at a time. They do not understand linking things together. The more people who have looked or who are trying to sell their house to buy a property, the better the chance of making things work. Thus while The Real Estate Agent actually makes the market work and tries to improve it, the 'sell your house first merchants' are actually depressing their own market, without realising it.

People do not want to sell not knowing where they are going. The casual, non-forced move is being discouraged. Worse still, these agents are not helping you, the public.

Chapter 8

Finding A House, Deciding On What To Offer, Negotiation

You want to move house, you have had your house valued by a Real Estate Agent so you know what you can afford. (If I have made you so distrustful of Estate Agents valuations, then why not pay for a professional valuation by a Chartered Surveyor who does not sell houses, and of the type described later, to value the property and then get the estate agents in and choose who you wish to market the property with the benefit of that advice.) or you have either sold and completed on your house and are in a position to proceed or that you have a buyer on your own house who is ready to proceed. Whichever way, you have got there; you are now in the position to place an offer on a property that the vendor of that property will know has a chance of coming to fruition.

I wish I had a pound for every time I have heard prospective purchasers tell me that they have been looking for a considerable period of time, they have been around many houses, seen the prices and they know what the values are. Oh dear, big mistake! They do not know what the values are. They know what the asking prices are and if the asking prices had been the value, in many cases, they would not have been available for them to look at as they would have been sold. We have established that to get properties on the market, many modern estate agents value high (and sell low) and if you are moving into a new area, how can you possibly know what the values are. There is, of course, greater knowledge now that sale prices are revealed by the Inland Revenue, but this can occasionally be misleading. The transactions may be internal and at a low level deliberately, one may have features that others didn't, sometimes the amount is wrong! Whilst extra real information of this type is to be welcomed, it is still not a substitute for the true professional valuer, working in an area and knowing his patch. You may say 'it will be valued by the Building Society'. You cannot and must not work off that valuation as a true valuation.

There are usually two situations:
1) You are buying with a mortgage and 2) you are buying for cash.

Where you are buying with a mortgage, your lender will require a valuation to be carried out to prove basically that their money is secure. Do not think of this as a valuation to tell you what the true value is. This is no longer the case. You have no control over who values the property and it will be carried out by a Company that is a 'panel Valuer'. The individual Surveyor/Valuer will be a member of The Royal Institute of Chartered Surveyors. Invariably today, the vast majority of building society/mortgage valuations are carried out by corporate surveyors who are basically employed by the banks. They will advise you if there are any major structural problems, but really the valuation they carry out is a tick-box exercise and is dependent upon whether the banks are lending mood, in which case they are more likely just to put the property through at the sale price, or if they don't want to lend, then they are just as likely to down value it, so that the sale cannot proceed. It is quite possible that these surveyors 1) come from miles away and don't know the local area, 2) are actually employed by the same company as you are getting the money from. Clearly you have to get your valuation done by the banks valuer but I would strongly recommend that you take independent advice, as already discussed and if you need a structural survey or homebuyer report, you get this done independently. Of course, this will increase the expense and it may be that you feel so comfortable with the price you are paying, that you say 'I would rather get it done by the corporate surveyor, as he does the mortgage valuation, for the sake of cost'. Fine, but if you have any doubt or are looking for help and guidance with regard to the price you are paying, do not rely on the panel valuers' valuation. The survey they can be held accountable for, the valuation is a far more difficult situation to prove.

Some independent Chartered Surveyors feel so strongly about this that they have formed an Independent Surveyors Association. It is worthwhile looking at their website and finding a local surveyor. They make the point that can these corporate surveyors be truly unbiased, when they are paid or indeed employed by the company lending the buyer the money. Importantly, the general public believe they are getting an independent valuation, when in fact they are not. Remember, they are working and being paid for by the proposed mortgagee, to tell them whether their money is secure, not whether you are paying the right price.

1) Where you are paying cash, you can of course dictate which type of survey or valuation you have, and more importantly who does it.

In essence, the Home Buyer Report should point out if a property has any major defects. This will then refer you to lots of tradesmen, damp & timber specialists, to get their opinion. The problem with that, of course, is that damp and timber specialists and builders do not make any money unless they find fault.

If you can afford it, I would suggest a Full Structural Survey and make sure that the surveyor does not, on the basis of the structure, put you on to other people, but will tell you himself what he believes the problems to be. I would expect him to refer, in terms of electrical, plumbing and heating to specialists, if there is a perceived problem, but not on the structure.

If you are moving locally, you may have a good feel of what local values are, but if you are moving out of the area into a new area, put simply, you have no chance. You can go around as many Estate Agents as you like getting their sales particulars and you will find that you don't know what the property will sell for and you will probably find a great variation in pricing, on the same type of property. As sales valuations varied when you sold your own property, so they will vary in the new area. Whether moving locally but particularly to a new area, you need help from a local Surveyor/Valuer, someone with no axe to grind and who knows his patch, and is on your side. They are becoming a rare breed, but they do still exist. Local Estate Agents may well be able to help you find one; certainly local solicitors will know which Surveyors generally give good advice and have a grip on the local values. Go and speak to them and say you are looking to buy a property and that prior to putting an offer in, you would like them to value the property. Most Valuers would probably do this for a fee of say £150 to £200 and if you then purchase, you will ask him to do the House Buyer Report/Survey that is then necessary. His Valuation Report does not need to be detailed. If it helps on a fee basis, it could even be done on a 'word of mouth' basis as if you purchase, he will be valuing it under the Home Buyer Report situation.

My advice is, do not use the Building Society Valuer for the Home Buyer Report, unless you are 100% sure of the value of the property.

When you are looking, the first question you ask an Estate Agent is 'How long has it been on the market'? The second question is 'Why are they selling'? The same question The Real Estate Agent would have asked you when he was valuing your property, to assess the whole situation. Within reason, look at properties that are beyond your affordability, but that are the type of property you want, particularly if they have been on the market for a long period of time. They are simply asking too much money and it may well be that the client will accept far less than the amount the property is on the market for. Within the previous two weeks of dictating this, my Company purchased a property for a client that was on the market for £385,000 for £300,000. This property was never re-advertised, but it was a probate situation, there were a number of beneficiaries and in that situation there is usually one of them that needs the money, plus the drop in price is split, so the hurt is not as great. Without re-advertising at a new price, it is ridiculous to drop that sort of money, but it was on the market for too much to start with, and may well have made more, had the Agents not killed it originally, or had they bothered to re-advertise it. They got it to sell (by the over valuation), they sold it, they got the fee!

When you have identified a property that you like, get your Valuer to have a look at it and report to you as to what the real value of the property is. The fact that you have had a valuation done and are spending money prior to making an offer, with a Chartered Surveyor, will encourage the vendors that you are serious, and that you have taken advice when you come in with a lower offer.

The other way of trying to purchase a property is to register an interest. You may feel uncomfortable putting in an offer that is affordable to you, which is so far below the asking price. You also run the risk of offending the purchaser who thinks his house is still worth what the Agent told him. If the vendor is in-situ, it is sometimes worth writing a letter to the Estate Agent. 'We absolutely loved the property and would love to purchase it, but we simply cannot afford the level at which it is on the market. If the price is reduced, or a lower offer is received, would you please keep us informed so that we can consider our situation at that time. Send a copy of the letter to the owners, if they live at the property.

'Dear Owner

Out of courtesy, please find a copy of the letter we have sent to your Estate Agents'.

The reason for this is that when the Agents get a far lower offer as in the above example, they do not necessarily go back, or tell people who register an interest weeks or months before. Thus in the above example, if the vendors knew of another interest they would make sure at least that the Agents contacted them, as many simply do not. We have an offer of £300,000, will you accept it – Yes and the people who have previously registered with them are not referred to, as per our example when The Real Estate Agent receives an offer.

The most important point here is that:-

1) You have received professional advice as to the true theoretical value for the property. Bear in mind that some properties will have different values to different purchasers, but you know what the base value is and then you can offer what the property is worth to you.

2) Where properties are overpriced, you are now in a position to offer at the correct level, or similarly where the properties are properly priced, offer at the correct level.

3) Where properties are on the market for too much money, you have registered an interest.

Basically the more straightforward you are when trying to purchase, the better. If you are asked for a 'best offer' in writing, then give it. If you have to pay a little too much to get the property of your dreams, then do it, but at least you know by how much you are doing it, because you have taken proper local valuation advice.

There are many types of negotiations that can take place. If you are in a bidding situation, the rule of thumb is basically decide the most you are prepared to go to, and be prepared to go up to it in stages. If you are fortunate enough that there is no other prospective purchaser after the property, then the Agent almost certainly will go backwards and forwards. Try not to get too emotional, do not be too positive that you really want the property and that this is the only property for you, if you have alternatives say so, but don't cut your nose off to spite your face either and lose the property you really want.

If you think about it, there is a case for having a professional person offer and negotiate on your behalf. If you are selling a house, most people will use an Estate Agent. The offer being made through an Estate Agent means that the Vendor has time to consider the offer and make an advised decision, without having the would-be purchaser opposite him. Yet would-be purchasers rush into Estate Agents offices full of excitement and enthusiasm and wearing their heart on their sleeve. Given that it is the Real Estate Agents duty and job to maximise the price, their body language gives away the fact that they will pay more for the property than they have offered. If negotiation is done by a third party i.e. a purchaser's Agent, then the personality of the offeree, the needs of the offeree, the emotional state of the offeree, is not known to the Vendor's Agent and it is so much less obvious, because the Real Estate Agent can judge the offeree merely by the amount and status of the offer on the table. We mentioned the surveyor on your side in earlier pages and it may well be worthwhile if you have used such an individual, to get him to do the offering for you. I believe there is a place for a service of conducting offers for prospective purchasers and whilst there would be a fee involved, it could save thousands of pounds in the long run.

However, you make your offer it should be subject to contract, and possibly, subject to survey.

As part of the equation, you will have to prove your affordability. This can be done in a number of ways in Real Estate Agencies, either by confirmation from your solicitor or by confirmation from your Bank or Mortgage Broker that a mortgage is arranged, or will be available. Under the Estate Agent Act, we have established that the Estate Agent has to 'qualify' the offer. In the early days, many corporate Agents would not put an offer forward unless a prospective purchaser had seen their qualifier. Their qualifier is of course a Mortgage Adviser and the whole idea of qualification was to try and sell the mortgage in-house.

It amazes me that you as a purchaser wanting to get a house as cheaply as possible, is necessarily expected willingly to tell the people who are acting for the vendor exactly what your financial situation is. In other words, once the qualifier or mortgage broker has seen you, that mortgage broker knows exactly what your affordability is. He is then able to tell the negotiator in the same Company, acting for the Vendor that you can afford a bit more. Giving them the information of exactly what you can afford, rather than a note from a separate Bank, that you can substantiate an offer you have made, means you have immediately undermined your negotiating position. This may seem a little bit extreme, and it may not always be of great importance but it is fact.

Where Mortgage Broking is done in-house, and you have competition against you for the purchase of a particular property and you feel that you may have been discriminated against because you did not place your mortgage with the Estate Agents broker, then simply tell the vendor. If you were not given the chance to give a 'best offer', if it was sold simply to a higher offer and you were never asked what level you would go to and, you would have gone higher, give the client and the agent in writing, a further offer. At no time go behind the Agent; duplicate everything where you know the address of the owner. Do not just acquiesce because another offer has been accepted simply because the Agent tells you a higher offer has been accepted; make sure the Vendor knows that at no time were you asked if you were prepared to increase your offer. If the vendor goes with the Agent there is nothing more to be done. If you do not know the whereabouts of the Vendor then there is nothing you can do about it.

Before making any offer, you will need to know what you can afford and you will need, therefore, mortgage advice. Maybe you can afford more than you are prepared to pay, which is a good way to be. The Estate Agent who acts as a Broker cannot discriminate against you, or should not discriminate against you, simply because you do not go with the Agent's in-house broker. I can hear many very good people who do everything properly, seething at these words, but if they need proof that this is an area of conflict of interest, (apart from a Channel 4 Dispatches undercover programme in 2014), I know of some purchasers who have gone to see the Agent's qualifier and actually go along with the company arranging a mortgage, until they have had their offer accepted. They then swap to another more suitable mortgage company simply because the Estate Agent arranging the mortgage can no longer refuse to sell to them just because they are using a different mode of finance. That shows that prospective purchasers are intimidated by the current situation. There is a conflict of interest and whereas many in-house brokers will completely do the job properly and be discreet, many simply will not. Indeed, who is the Agent's duty of care to? Their company is acting for the vendor. Many people often comment in these Agencies, that the staff appears to be more interested in selling financial services, than selling houses. In many cases, that is how they are targeted.

Independent Mortgage Brokers are a dying breed, largely because the FSA and the Banks want them that way. They are, however, a resourceful lot despite every disadvantage that is put in their way, some still survive.

Independent Mortgage Brokers are that, and they can search the market and get you the most appropriate deal. More importantly they are usually not linked to any particular life company, so that when you come to get advice on life cover, you also get a broad spectrum. There is little point in getting a nice cheap mortgage and then being linked to a life company as part of the deal that then costs you more.

If you go direct to a Bank then they will usually only offer you their own mortgage product and they can also only offer you their own linked life company's products. Take independent advice which should then be able to go anywhere. The Independent Mortgage Broker is also used to problems and will help solve them. If you have difficulties along the way, he is on your side rather than acting for the particular bank involved. We have seen Bank's suddenly change the criteria shortly before exchange of contracts in recent years. You need someone fighting on your side, who knows the rights and wrongs.

By whatever means you have decided, you want to buy the house and you want to offer. My advice is to decide the maximum the property is worth to you, which may or may not be the same as what you can afford.

Usually, you would offer below the maximum and be prepared to go to that figure, in stages. There is no absolute way to negotiate. Some do it easily; some are straightforward, some are not.

Chapter 9

The Offer is Accepted

You have managed to negotiate a price that is agreeable to the vendor, through his Agent; your offer has been accepted 'Subject to Contract': this merely means that either party can withdraw from the agreement, until such time as the Solicitors exchange contracts without financial penalty. Your Solicitor has been put in touch with the Vendor's Solicitor by the Agent. They have accepted that your mortgage is in place and that you are ready to proceed. If your offer is subject to your viable sale, then the Real Estate Agent who is acting for you on your sale, will expect to give full information and details of that chain to your Vendor's Agent. He should give you every assistance to ensure that any offer you place is fully understood. He should have up-to-date information for you as to the progress of your chain and help you to secure your new property. The next step can be:-

Chapter 10

Re-Negotiation

The Building Society valuation can cause a problem if the property down values. In other words, the valuer indicates that the purchase price you have agreed is too high and if for example, you were borrowing 75% of the valuation figure, the amount you can borrow is now reduced as the house has down valued from the price you agreed.

It may be that having got your survey report you find that there are more defects than you realised and the cost of putting these right in order to obtain the loan is such that you cannot afford to pay the amount you have offered, in good faith.

Reductions in price are clearly not popular but again, your purchase price is dictated by your affordability which may be out of your hands, or indeed it may be that money you had set aside to do certain other jobs, are now going to have to be used to pay for immediate necessary repairs.

It is a good idea to give the report or important sections of the report, to the Estate Agent you are dealing with. This means he can highlight the situation to his vendor and also, if he is a Surveyor and a Real Estate Agent, comment on the report in a useful way. In a sense, these negotiations are more informed than the original negotiations.

There is now a professional valuation and there is also professional advice as to the immediate work required. The vendor will take a view and often, with common sense and a little relaxation of price, the deal goes ahead but at a lower level. It may be that there is a chain involved. Say there is an estimate of £9,000 of unexpected costs and you can contribute £2,500 but no more. It may be that to get their property sold and moved, the two other people above you are prepared to reduce their prices by £3,500 each, which means the difference between their houses selling and them getting moved and getting on with life or not. The advantage of the same agent being involved in the chain throughout is obvious, but it may be your agent has to deal through other agents or solicitors, who have need to speak to their own clients.

Nevertheless, by pushing the boundaries and thinking outside the box, the Real Estate Agent can make things happen. Otherwise, the sale may simply have failed.

Chapter 11

The Legal Process

In many ways the legal process, whilst entirely necessary, should be a formality. The property has been purchased before and therefore, its title should be good and if it has been sold since 1987, then the title will be registered. When you are purchasing, your Solicitor has to act far more vigilantly than on the sale, since when you want to move again, you will have to sell the property that he has allowed you to buy.

The Real Estate Agent always tries to have a good relationship with Solicitors. It is important not to harry them but to keep in touch with them and make sure there is a line of communication if there is a chain situation. The Real Estate Agent will try and find out who the Solicitors and purchasers are in the entire chain, so that he can ring any one at any time to find out how the chain if progressing, especially when people are wanting to complete. The Real Estate Agent needs to have an understanding of the legal process as he can then understand and react to what is happening if necessary, when there are problems. The Estate Agent may be asked to re-define plans that are incorrect, to measure

127

boundaries. A professional eye can help the situation to progress.

There is no doubt that lenders are requiring more and more information: a conservatory built 10 years ago which has no Certificate may now create a problem.

This perceived risk can be insured against and another £150 to £200 goes into some Company's pocket for no real reason, apart from the fact that the Lenders that make the rules probably own the insurance companies. More recently, some lenders are requiring that the mortgage deed is prepared by their own panel solicitor. Thus the local solicitor is again under pressure and I am sure this panel solicitor or more likely licensed company will probably be prepared to do the conveyancing as well.

It is important to keep in touch with your Solicitor during the conveyancing process.

Often they will send contracts out and when asked, after four weeks, will say they have had nothing back. The Real Estate Agent will ring the purchaser's Solicitor and ask him if that is the case and if so, why have they not made enquiries? It is important to keep up the momentum.

The normal time between sale and completion used to be about two and a half months. It is more like an average of 3 ½ to 4 ½ months in 2016.

With the Real Estate Agent gently keeping the pressure on your Solicitor, making sure replies and communications are being dealt with in a timely manner, you will COMPLETE THE PURCHASE OF YOUR HOUSE. THE REAL ESTATE AGENT HAS COMPLETED HIS JOB – HE HAS MOVED YOU.

SECTION III – RANDOM THOUGHTS

Chapter 12

Revealing Offers

It is not often I agree with the Consumers Association, but in keeping with the modern requirement of 'transparency', they believe that all offers should be revealed. In other words, if you are asking £100,000 and the Agent receives an offer of £95,000, the Agent should tell the person offering, viewing or wanting to place an offer, that you have received an offer of £95,000, not that you have an undisclosed offer but you are asking £100,000. I think the decision should be left to the vendor and certainly most purchasers prefer to know, and remember, they may also be a Vendor. Yet the Code of Practice for the Property Ombudsman Scheme, also followed by the Chartered Surveyors, says that the amount of offers shall not be revealed. Why? Why not give a Vendor the option, which he has in law? What difference does it make?

Where it makes a difference is that it makes it easier for the Agent to manipulate a situation towards a certain buyer, if he does not reveal offers. That is the reason for not revealing offers, in the Code of Practice operated by the Ombudsmen Scheme. You have to be a member of some form of redress scheme to become an Estate Agent. The Ombudsman Scheme was basically created by the corporate companies some 25 years ago. It was created to give respectability to the great lie that they were for the public good, and to disguise all those occasions referred to as Conflict of Interest, when the Agent is selling to a client for whom the Agent is also arranging a mortgage, hence he is getting paid by both the vendor and purchaser. As part of their little wheeze, they came up in the Code of Practice with the mandate 'You shall not reveal an offer', they never said why, nor have they ever said why, nor have they ever said 'You should take your client's instructions' pointing out the various benefits and disadvantages etc. Here is the reason why they do not want to reveal offers: you are asking £100,000 for a property, you get an offer from Purchaser A of £95,000, Purchaser B comes along and also wishes to make an offer. As Agent, you say the asking price is £100,000 and we have an offer, but we are not going to tell you what it is, please place an offer. Purchaser B puts in an offer of £94,000; Purchaser B has a mortgage already arranged and if he moves to another company, he will have to pay the penalty of a redemption payment. Purchaser A has offered more, but will take a mortgage with the agent company. Technically the Agent is doing nothing wrong; he has put the offers in writing, he has revealed to the client there is an offer of £94,000 and one of £95,000, which would you like to take? Believe me, a lot of clients are very naïve, they are so grateful for an offer which will allow them to move, they will not ask the appropriate questions, or tell the Agent to go back to purchaser B and ask him for more, or they will assume the Agent has already done this. The Agent, on instruction sells at £95,000, he gets the mortgage, he tells Purchaser B his offer has been declined and the property sold for a higher figure. Sound familiar? If he had revealed that the offer in was £95,000 then the purchaser would at least have known, and may well have offered £96,000. Thus, had the Agent revealed the offer, it would be more difficult to manipulate the situation towards those buyers who will take a mortgage out with him. You will say 'surely this does not happen, not in nice big corporate companies run by banks and the like'. The staff are targeted on Financial Services and where their friends and colleagues get more money if a certain buyer gets it. We are talking about companies whose doctrine is to maximise their business, not do what is right for the client, as discussed before. Of course it happens every day. (Since this was written, an undercover Channel 4 Dispatches programme exposed the practice in a major Corporate Estate Agency).

As a Real Estate Agent, if you do think that you wish to reveal offers, there is no doubt that it makes for harder work. Agents that do not reveal offers tend to go for 'best and final offers' more quickly. We have three people wanting to buy, ask for their 'best and final offer'. They do not get embroiled in a bidding situation, with a lot more telephone calls and also stress for the Agent involved, but in many ways it is the fairest way of negotiating, as everybody knows what the offer is. To those prospective purchasers who say to The Real Estate Agent, 'I don't believe you have another offer', the response is rule of thumb, 'well don't put a higher offer in and see whether we sell it'. The Real Estate Agent does not invent offers and knows that it is hard enough to remember and document all the offers that have come into a busy office, never mind inventing them.

Usually those Agents that do not reveal offers simply will say that there has been a higher offer. The prospective purchaser, who understands negotiation, merely then has to keep increasing his offer and asking 'will that be enough', but most are comparatively inexperienced and would not know to do this.

I cannot see any reasonable reason to objecting to revealing offers. If an offer is far below the asking price, then the Real Estate Agent may feel it better not to reveal it; he may feel that the next prospective purchaser is going to offer nearer the asking price and therefore best not to reveal it, but that is within his discretion. There are times when revealing a low offer will get the bidding started. People offering give confidence in the value of the property and all of a sudden you find that it has swept past the asking price and is going into territory that you only hoped it would get to. Would this have happened if a high asking price had been put on it? Very probably not. Bidding gives confidence that there is someone else out there prepared to pay the price. The purchasers may have gone to the Bank of Mum & Dad and borrowed another ten thousand pounds, because having seen the house, they have fallen in love with it, but they would not have looked at it, had it been priced higher. Having seen the property, it has stopped being just about money and is about buying a home. The emotional part of the transaction has kicked in!

I am not saying that there is an absolute right or wrong way, but if you don't reveal an offer, then the person offering is going blind and does not know where to pitch it. There's a chance he will pitch it below and not be told, just that the house is sold to a higher offer. If he is told what the offer is, he has the decision to make an offer above it. In the Real Estate Agents contract, it specifically reserves the right to reveal offers to prospective purchasers and thus, whilst not in line with the Ombudsman Scheme Code of Practice and also the Code of Practice for Chartered Surveyors, which for some unexplained reason, have adopted a similar stance, he has told his Vendor that this is what he intends to do, and he cannot be held accountable for the supposed breach of the Code of Practice, which is entirely within the law. Of course, with many modern estate agents' policy of over pricing, they rarely get more than one person interested at the same time and when they do eventually sell the property, they often sell it for less than the Real Estate Agents value, and less than if had they priced it properly in the first place.

One of the greatest advantages of asking for 'Offers in the Region of' while placing it realistically and revealing offers when you get competition is that it allows you flexibility. If in actual fact the interest tells you that you have placed the property too low, then providing you get people there, it really doesn't matter because competition will take it up. This is particularly true of character properties or properties where you know there is a high general demand. The property will bid to the general affordability given in the theoretical value, however sometimes it will also result in the property going above the theoretical value when two people particularly want it.

Had the property been originally priced so far beyond its general affordability and theoretical value, then those people most probably would not have looked at it and bidding would not have happened. In a sense, it is a marketing exercise, and in a time of reasonable demand pricing is only critical if you over price and stop people going to the property.

Chapter 13

The Free Valuation

The free valuation is here to stay, yet to the Real Estate Agent, it is a professional exercise, a professional valuation. He therefore puts the same effort into getting it right, as though he were an expert witness going to court, because he wants to do the best for his client. Once, people paid for valuations, even if they were going to sell their house. The valuation fee was then reimbursed, by a reduction in commission. Then came the business men into Estate Agency and the free valuation was born. Common sense will tell you that nothing is free. 'Free valuation' became a pitch to get the property onto the market and an opportunity to sell the services of the Estate Agent. The implications of over valuation, properties standing on the market, a reduction in transaction levels, all stem in part from the 'free valuation'. There is a perception amongst the public that when an Agent goes to the property he is actually selling his services and, of course, to a point he is, but the Real Estate Agent is trying to give correct professional advice. People will say, 'I want you to be realistic' to which the Real Estate Agent replies, 'I will give you what I believe to be the right valuation and then discuss asking price and what we are trying to achieve and take instructions'.

If the free valuation is not totally ideal to the selling public, it is a disaster to the Real Estate Agent. If people had to pay for a property valuer's time, they would not get six Estate Agents out. This frequently happens and eight times out of ten, the decision is made, not on the knowledge or ability of the person valuing, nor the apparent services offered by the particular firm, but on the amount of valuation placed on the property and the asking price proposed. This means that instead of one or two Estate Agents attending the property, now many more are attending and thus all Estate Agents having opted for free valuations, spend half their time doing abortive work. Worse, for the Real Estate Agent, they are following other people around, often with no local knowledge whatsoever, giving correct advice and getting absolutely nothing for it.

You probably do not realise just how far valuations are 'out'. You may think £20,000, £30,000 or £50,000. Particularly in one-off rural properties, they can be hundreds of thousands out. At the time of dictating this, three properties have sold which were valued by my company.

Property A. valued at £520,000/£540,000 with a maximum asking price of £545,000, placed on the market at £625,000 systematically reduced and then sold for £500,000 after fifteen months.

Property B. placed on the market, valued at £530,000/£540,000, placed on the market at £625,000, sold for £510,000.

Property C. valued by my company at £380,000/£400,000 in November 2010, placed on the market at £550,000, sold for £381,000 in November 2011.

In all the above cases, the reduced asking price was very close to £100,000 more than the sale price.

The Real Estate Agent alludes to this phenomenon when he is carrying out his free valuation. He is told the prospective vendors want him to be realistic, and then watches as it goes on the market at some ridiculous figure. Small wonder that the market does not work and small wonder that people actually give up looking to sell, if their move is not enforced, as they perceive they will have to have their house on the market for anything up to five years to sell it. Not only that, but the realistic public think they will not be able to afford to move, as they cannot afford the prices. The Agents are killing their own market and they are so short-sighted that they don't see it.

From the professional Valuers' point of view, the shame is that this means a denigration of the art and science of valuation. Small wonder that professional valuation has become far less appreciated since many of the parties doing it, are carrying it out with a complete lack of integrity. The professional Valuers' time is no longer appreciated. People come to you wanting everything for free. 'Just have a look at this, just have a look at that, just give a quick off the top of your head valuation.' The professional Valuer cannot do that, not consistently and get it right. If you are going to do the job properly, you need to take time and have comparable evidence, and local knowledge and experience, and with computers, so much more evidence is readily available to allow you to do the job even better than ever before. The Real Estate Agent has ended up competing against 'off the top of their head' merchants and the appreciation of his general expertise has diminished.

There are other ways in which the free valuation has become a scourge to the Real Estate Agent. Where people need to know the value of their property but do not want to sell it, they will ring Estate Agents and ask them to come and do a valuation for sale. People feel quite morally able to ask Estate Agents to value their property on false pretences. Amazingly, some Solicitors have become complicit in this, notably in situations of divorce and probate.

In divorce situations there are instances where the property is not to be sold, but to be purchased by one of the parties. In recent years, in many cases, I have arrived to find out from the so called prospective Vendor that the Solicitor had advised to get three sale valuations and take a mean, to settle the price to be paid. The stupidity of this is pretty plain to see. If the solicitor is advising the party purchasing, he will not get a proper valuation, but three pitches to get it on the market and the mean of that will be above the going market value. All this to save a professional fee of say £250 and, to get it right first time.

Probate valuations have to be carried out by a Chartered Surveyor and it should be a Red Book Valuation. Yet again, some solicitors suggest people get three sale

139

valuations and take a mean, as to the property's value. It is just an indication of how free valuations have made the professional estate agent's time unimportant. It is amazing that when you get to these properties and you find out the real reason why you are there, and you say you will do the valuation but you will charge a fee, people are indignant. The free valuation has meant that your time is not valued by the general public and they feel it is their right to have a free valuation done, even though you are going to get absolutely no financial reward for giving them your expertise and your time.

Ultimately there is no such thing as 'a free lunch'. I have seen people completely confused and amazed at the differences between so called valuations, particularly in country properties, where a range of £150,000 - £200,000 is common, in £400,000 - £500,000 properties.

Of course, property portal providers do provide estimates, often known as Automated Valuation Model (AVM) and some Internet Only Estate Agents rely on these as they are often operating from bases far from the property they are proposing to sell. These estimates are based on data the Portals gather in the general course of their business and the sale prices subsequently recorded and published by the Land Registry. I do not dismiss them, indeed the modern Valuer will use the information to assist him, but complete reliance on them is dangerous, as it is a blanket approach and values can vary considerably even in a distance of some 3 – 5 miles, due to local considerations that only local knowledge can take account of. Often, they are just plainly wrong.

So how do members of the public sieve through the chaff? Of course have faith in your own judgement, but most certainly, if you are getting probate or divorce valuations, then you should pay for a professional valuation, carried out by a Chartered Surveyor with good local knowledge. If you are selling then you could probably get a valuation for sale purposes from a Chartered Surveyor for £150 to £200. I do not mean a Chartered Surveyor who also sells houses I mean an independent Chartered Surveyor and local Valuer, who does not sell houses. He has no axe to grind, but acts for purchasers in the local market and knows the local values. He will therefore be able to give you an appropriate valuation. You can get your free valuation from the Estate Agents and make your decision as to which agent to use, in the light of their individual appeal, fees etc. but also on the basis of a true valuation. Such a course of action would save a lot of people an awful lot of wasted time and heartache.

Once you have your professional valuation, you can then ask whatever asking price you want, with whichever Agent you want, but you are doing so in full knowledge of the real value.

Chapter 14

House Price Increase – The Cause

Is there a topic which is more written about and debated in the British media than British house prices? Hardly a day passes without a headline in some paper of prices having increased or decreased, by whatever miniscule proportion. Why such attention is given to these short term figures I never understand, since hardly any of the institutions or building societies that produce them, give figures that agree. More meaningless is the detail of how much money has been lent by these institutions, as they rarely differentiate between re-mortgaging or for the purchase of property, or indeed new build.

There is no doubt that if these figures are positive over a 6/12 month period, that they do give confidence to the buying public and confidence is paramount as people are less enthusiastic to perhaps venture into the housing market, if they think prices are going to reduce.

The common media preoccupation is to come up with all sorts of reasons why houses prices will or will not rise. They quote low economic growth, lack of spending power in the household budget. Of course, all these things do affect house prices, but only in a minor way. It should be remembered that at the end of the day, people have to live in a house.

The advent of the rental market and the availability of good quality housing for rent, has confused the issue slightly, but the simple fact has always been that there is always a high demand for British housing, although I believe the current 'Help to Buy' scheme and mass construction of houses being currently built, is changing that in some less prosperous and populated areas. After living expenses, there is an amount in the family budget which can be put towards paying a mortgage. If people's income increases then there is more disposable income for house purchase. If the Bank's leave the multiples the same between income and the amount they will lend on a property, then house inflation depends upon the increase in income of the public. Simple.

However, if they change the multiple or lending criteria, then it affects values. Thus in the late '80s we had huge inflation because the banks increased their lending ratio from 2½ to 4½ times salary (there were other changes in lending criteria as well). Again in 2002, they did exactly the same thing. Very simply, around June 1st 2002, a prospective buyer has a £20,000 deposit, he is earning £30,000 and is told he can borrow 3 ½ times salary. He can offer £125,000 for a property. On June 30th he is told he can borrow 5 times salary. He can offer £165,000 for the house. It is the same house, but if he didn't do it, someone else would and so everybody had to pay more for the same house. In June 2002, if you were out of the market, living in rented accommodation, you were £20,000 down overnight. In 2002, in the area I worked, prices rose 30% and the Agent who overvalued at the beginning of the year, was proved right by the end of it.

The reason for this was so that the Banks made more money. With increasing prosperity, there was an increase in household income and people had more disposable income to spend. All the banks have to do is increase the multiple and it means people can afford more for the property. It meant everybody could afford more for property and the trouble was, unless the buying public paid it, they simply did not get the house. They didn't have a chance to purchase, unless they paid the increased amount they could afford, as somebody else who wanted the house could afford it too. So with all the economist's reasons, the reason for house inflation is really very simple; it will increase according to the amount of household budgets or if the banks suddenly decide to change the lending criteria.

The result of the banks activity which has been referred to as 'Commerce without Conscience' means instead of the public having money to spend on the high street and increase everybody's wealth and prosperity, we have to pay twice as much in mortgage interest, to live in exactly the same house as we would have done had the banks not increased the lending multiple. The banks, simply by their lending policies, diverted money from peoples' income that should have gone elsewhere in the economy, giving the British public a higher standard of living directly to them. It makes mis-selling PPI pale into insignificance.

Chapter 15

House Price Decrease – The Cause

In 1990, there was a vicious rise in interest rates, which today is almost incomprehensible. Interest rates rose from approximately 8 ½% to around 15%. In the North of England, mainly people borrowed only up to 3 ½ times salary but in the South of England where there was more disposable income, the Banks allowed them to borrow as much as 4 ½ times salary. As interest rates rose, particularly in the South, people found it impossible to make the repayments. They were therefore forced to put their properties on the market and the Banks, in an arbitrary manner, reduced the multiple that people could borrow to 3% from 4½%. The result was negative equity overnight. Instead of saying to the next person who was going to borrow to try to buy the house, 'look at your affordability and your lifestyle' they simply reduced the multiple, which then reduced the amount the would-be purchaser could afford to pay. House prices dropped and the people they had encouraged to borrow 4 ½ times salary, very simply lost money in the sale of their house. It was the change of lending criteria that caused the drop in value. As prices rose during the '90s at a rate of something like 10% every three years, the next boom was to be to in 2002/2003 rising to October 2007. As the Banks did not have any integrity with regard to mortgage lending, it turned out they did not have any integrity with regard to other matters either and so came the credit crunch.

As house price bubbles were caused by changing the lending criteria, in those cases the lending multiple, if you wanted to drastically reduce your lending, then there is one easy way to do it. The Banks simply demanded that those buying, who had previously been asked for no deposit or say 5%, were suddenly asked for 30%: if you want to kill a market that is the way to do it. If you want to suddenly drastically reduce lending to the house buying public that is the way to do it. In 2008 the Banks basically said, 'we are not going to lend to people who want to buy a house, unless they have a large deposit'. Even then the number of mortgage packages on the market was reduced hugely. The whole housing market came to a stop in a manner which is completely unprecedented. All of a sudden the First Time Buyer, who in the normal market starts everything going, was unable to get a deposit together, large enough to enable them to buy. Furthermore, with more people having to rent, so rental values increased, with the result that more family income was being spent on rent than would have been paid on a mortgage. Higher rents paid to live in a property meant the would-be First Time Buyer found it impossible to save. The large deposit required by the Banks had a tremendous downward effect on the prices that could be paid and therefore the value for the First Time Buyer house. The traditional First Time Buyer house was at a value, depending upon area, of say £95,000 to £125,000 (please bear in mind we are not talking about the London area here). If a First Time Buyer property did sell, it sold at £30,000 to £40,000 less than its peak value, which meant that the house he bought made £30,000 to £40,000 less than peak value and so on up the chain. The Real Estate Agent would say to clients 'if you get less you pay less' and thus hopes to make the chains work. Whilst it is easy to make chains work on a rising market, it is very much more difficult on a decreasing market.

There are, of course, local variations, but where people live, work and stay in an area and more particularly, do not move too for retirement or holiday home purposes, where cash was still often not available, this is what happened in the immediate aftermath of the credit crunch. It became extremely difficult to sell houses and when you did sell them, they were well below peak values. As mortgage lending eased the market improved and prices rallied.

Chapter 16

How Estate Agents Affect Housing Transaction Levels

Set out below is the number of housing transactions of established houses, not new build in England and Wales from the 1980s until 2006. Look at it for a minute. There is no doubt, boom and bust in the housing market has been caused by the banks' policies. When house prices are rising, it is comparatively easy to sell a house and if you overvalue it, by the end of the year the price has caught up. It is very much easier to sell houses on a rising market because the effect of over valuation disappears. In the 1987 and 1988 and 2002 and 2003, the volume of house transactions peaked at the same time as the Banks increased the multiples of income to loan, thus nullifying the need for agents to make the market.

There is something underlying there. If you look at the volume of house transactions in 1988, it was 2 million, what the chart does not say is that that represented 15% of the housing stock in England and Wales with people moving house every 7 years. It peaks again in 2002/2003 at 1.4 million transactions in England and Wales, yet this figure was achieved nearly every year in the 1980s.

This graph features commercial transactions which make up approximately 10% of the total sales.

Table 40 **Numbers of mortgage advances per year in Great Britain**

Thousands

	1980	1985	1990	1991	1992	1993	1994	1995	1996	1997	1998	1999	2000	2001	2002	2003
Building societies	675	1,073	780	661	531	561	602	513	589	396	230	304	311	225	247	197
+ Banks		176	333	316	327	397	359	346	431	674	678	757	734	965	1,061	967
+ Insurance companies	18	19	26													
+ Local authorities	16	23	8													
+ Other specialist lenders				83	38	34	52	50	65	116	127	82	68	68	113	202
= Total	709	1,291	1,147	1,060	896	992	1,013	909	1,085	1,186	1,035	1,143	1,113	1,257	1,422	1,365

Sources: Housing and Construction Statistics (annual volumes) for 1980 to 1990; Bank of England 1991 onwards.

Notes: The 1980 figures are for England and Wales only and exclude council house sales. Thereafter, figures are for Great Britain, and include council house sales. Abbey National Plc figures included with the banks figures from July 1989. The Bank of England data from 1991 onwards also reflects the continuing trend for building societies to convert to banks. The figures for banks and other specialist lenders for the years 1991 to 1997 are understood to include remortgage advances as well as loans for house purchase. From 1998 the data relates solely to advances for house purchase.

What it does not tell you is that 1.4 million represented 5% of the existing housing stock with people moving house every 17 years. Why the change? Why did people not move house as often at the time in 2006 when mortgage rates had never been lower and mortgages more available or affordable? The economist will come up, no doubt, with all sorts of money reasons but they do not hold water.

I repeat, mortgage availability was just as great, in 2002 as in 1988, interest rates were far lower, so why are people not moving house as often? The economist will give other reasons, job mobility perhaps, but again it does not hold water.

The reason is very simple – the demise of the 'Real Estate Agent'

After 1988, much of the professional skill required to make the market work had disappeared. Bought out by corporate chains, the skill people required had largely gone. If you over value, you stop a market. Putting chains together and selling four houses at a time is not possible if you overvalue. If it takes you 9 months to sell each house in a chain of four that equates to 3 years, people have died or divorced in that time! As they could not value accurately and 'Listers' were targeted as to the number of properties they got on the market, it became unheard of to take a property off the market where there was a property to sell. Previously, this had been done and chains created where the next house in the chain was just as saleable as the previous house, as it had been properly valued. The

Real Estate Agent could no longer make chains work because some 'valuer' would tell a person in the chain that their house was worth more than it was and the chain did not come together. Agents came up with the idea of telling people to sell their house first and go into rented accommodation, not knowing where they were going to end up and how much they were going to have to pay. Not only that, due to a lack of understanding of how the market works, the corporate bosses and the new breed of Estate Agents were still telling valuers to list at any price, it will sell eventually, keep up our market share!

The general public do not like uncertainty; where they see houses on the market for months and sometimes years, they think twice about moving themselves. Where people wanted to move to a bigger house, they simply extended. Instead of estate agent's boards on estates it was then the domain of builder's boards, extending. There is only one way to carry out estate agency and that is properly. If you don't do it properly things don't work. If you don't value with integrity, then it comes back to bite you. Thus the corporate agents with their bosses in glass houses and many modern private Estate Agents have helped to kill their own market by giving poor advice and not having staff who actually understand the job. The effect of the corporate onslaught of estate agency has been to reduce the number of Real Estate Agents and dramatically reduce the number of transactions within the country. Had the Real Estate Agents been in business in great number in 2006, it is far more likely that 15% of the existing housing stock would have changed hands in 2006 with everybody still moving every 7 years. Agents as well as economic circumstances, make markets.

Oh! And the Estate Agents themselves would have made more money, as Agents make money overall by the number of houses they sell, not by the prices they achieve, the Mortgage Broker would have brokered more mortgages and the banks would have made more loans. Madness!

The modern idea that estate agency is all about sales people and not about professional people is flawed. The most obvious example is where a Real Estate Agent can save a sale of a property that has had an adverse survey, by looking at the report and putting the highlighted problems, that often look so bad in the written word into perspective. A sales only person cannot do that and another potential transaction is lost.

In recent years the credit crunch has brought another dimension to transaction numbers reducing to 600,000. If people can't borrow money then they can't buy houses, but even today, people are being told figures which are simply not achievable given the current circumstances.

Remember the job is about moving people and if a person gets less for his house then they must pay less for the next one. It is the differential that is important. A real estate agent will tell people what their house would have been valued at peak and what it is worth now, the vendor then makes a decision as to how to proceed with regard to the asking price. Houses currently are still being placed on the market as though there has been no reduction and so everything stagnates. That transaction levels should reach a figure of under a million is a national disgrace. The restriction of human movement is not a good thing for any economy. People spend money when they move house and they have a right to aspire to larger properties, smaller properties etc. The credit crunch is obviously the reason for the current massive drop but it does not explain why people are moving every 17 years in 2002 as opposed to every 7 in 1988. Small areas, where you have good Estate Agents, have upheld transaction levels because the advice is right. The reason transaction levels have slumped is because of poor estate agency, and poor advice, resulting in houses being overpriced and staying on the market for years. It is basically down to lack of integrity and the Real Estate Agent is caught in the middle of this, carrying out more and more valuations but seeing the business go elsewhere for being right, with the eventual sale price often below his valuation. With transaction levels at approximately 500,000 and 600,000 in the year 2012, 500-600,000 from 2 million in 1988 with many more houses built, it is little wonder the coalition Government felt it had to act with the 'Help to Buy' scheme. You may argue it had nothing to do with the low number of transactions; people unable to move, get into a retirement home, get close to the grandchildren, or get into a bungalow because they couldn't climb the stairs anymore, and more to do with bailing out the corporate builders.

These are politicians after all.

Chapter 17

Banks Lending & the Link to Housing Transaction Levels

I attach a graph showing the number of residential housing transactions within England and Wales as available. You can see that when lending criteria stayed the same, there was little variation in the number of transactions. Increases and decreases were steady and more akin to a growth of prosperity. However, the areas that should be marked were 1986 to 1989 and 2002 to 2007, during which time the Banks dramatically increased the lending multiples, and brought in interest only mortgages and other means of allowing people to borrow more. The effect on the transaction levels can be seen and correlates to the increase in prices. It is interesting that transaction levels should rise at the same time as prices so dramatically. This is because the over valuation carried out by so many Estate Agents, is very simply overhauled by the price increase during the year and made property easier to sell. Thus in 2002 where I believe there was 30% inflation, transaction levels increased dramatically as by the end of that year, the property would sell for what the over valuing Estate Agent had put it on the market for. In 2008, the effect of the credit crunch and the Banks change in lending criteria and the requirement for a large deposit, meant that it was not just a case of not being able to pay a purchase price, the would be First Time Buyer simply could not get a mortgage.

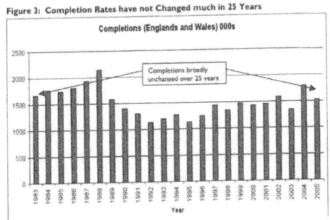

Figure 3: Completion Rates have not Changed much in 25 Years

Source: Negotiator – April 2008

I simply do not understand why this has not been understood more widely. At that stage, before the credit crunch, repossessions were at a normal level, and the increased number of repossessions have taken place more due to the credit crunch, since it was that which made many people unable to meet their mortgage repayments. In other words, it was the Banks other activities that caused the demise of many home owners, and consequent repossessions. By changing the lending criteria, they have dropped values and; they have therefore made less secure the properties they have already lent money on. If a property had to be repossessed, the would-be buyer could not afford what would have been paid for it with money supplied by the same banks. Whilst they may have been trying to make their lending more secure on one hand, they were making what they had already lent on, far less secure on the other, and will have lost money on those repossessions. In the meantime, in 2009 transaction levels dropped to 600,000 and 2010 was little better.

We discussed housing transactions earlier and implicated the effect where people move less often because of poor management of the market, in times when there was a good provision of mortgage availability and affordability. However, in this instance, the normal First Time Buyer was simply stopped from buying a property. The number and type of houses that were selling plummeted and were selling in many cases to Buy to Let investors. The ability of even the Real Estate Agent to make this market work, was tested to the extreme and his chance of keeping market share, when he was telling people their houses was worth £30,000 to £40,000 less than they had been at peak, was minimal. Other agents would still say the property was worth what it had been at peak and transaction levels crashed. Where the Real Estate Agent could get instructions, he could only piece chains together if his clients would work on the basis of if 'you get less but you pay less'. This is very much harder to make people understand, than the situation where in times of high inflation, you get more but you pay more.

Chapter 18

The Human Effect of Banks' Lending Policies

We have discussed transaction levels and prices affected by the Banks' lending policies, but what has been the real human effect? The real cost to the British public of the effect of the credit crunch, and the change of lending criteria brought in without any real thought, is basically to make prisoners of people in their own homes. Very simply, human movement has been severely curtailed, apart from very wealthy honey pot areas, aided and abetted by unscrupulous Estate Agents over valuing to keep market share. The large deposit has meant that it is not simply a case of reducing prices; even if you reduce prices, there is not the number of people out there to buy, as nobody can get started because of the requirement for a large deposit.

The effect on the long suffering general public is largely unmentioned. People move at different stages of their lives and perhaps the worst people affected are the elderly and infirm. Widows who have lost their husbands living in a substantial house, are unable to sell and unable to keep it, in practical terms from cutting the grass and in financial terms, in paying the bills. People who would like to move jobs, do not feel able to do so because they are frightened that they would not be able to sell their house, or have to live away from the family home for a long period of time. The elderly who wish to live nearer to their children or grandchildren, cannot do so because they cannot sell their house. Families who have outgrown their current property cannot move and those who wish to better their lifestyle cannot do so. These various human situations are evident the length and breadth of the country and the prime reason is that Banks have caused house price inflation to make money, and then caused massive house price deflation in order to (as they see it) safeguard their position.

If people do have to sell, they are looking at losing a considerable amount of money. They would have to sell if at all possibly at a huge discount, but buy at a much smaller discount. The theory of 'if you get less you pay less' works to a degree but not if there is an almost' enforced sale' situation, in terms of time perhaps because as an older person there is a real need to move quickly.

To me this is a far greater scandal than PPI or any mis-selling. Instead of treating housing as a social issue, the Banks have treated it as a money-making situation and caused terrible hardship, and influenced the mobility of the British public.

Whereas Building Societies used to look to the good of their members, the Banks have looked to the good of their shareholders and the short term gain. The fact is that the United Kingdom has the highest house prices in the world.

It is no accident, it has been caused by the bank's lending criteria and an increase in the multiple of income to loan.

In the late '80s, High Street banks lent on approximately 15% of all housing transactions. In 2008, it was nearer 90%. The change of Building Societies to Banks and takeovers and mergers has caused this. The High Street Banks have shown a cynical disregard for the good of public interest in many ways, but in my view, nothing is worse than the cynical way they have treated the British house-owning public. It begs the question, should they ever have been allowed to get into lending on residential property and should they be allowed to do so without tighter regulation in the future. The limitation of the multiple of income to loan by the Governor of the Bank of England is a start, but I feel much more will be required.

In the meantime, the limitation or lack of funding for house purchase and the inability of people to move house, was being noticed at last by the government. Lobbied by the large corporate builders, which having taken over so many smaller local building companies now found themselves in the position that they have built so many new, particularly starter homes, that they could not sell. During 2012 – 2013 there were substantial calls in the press from corporate builders, saying that they could not sell their homes because of the lack of availability of mortgages. Another question is brought to bear, in the heading of the next chapter.

Chapter 19

Help To Buy – Who Has It Really Helped?

If proof were needed of how changes in lending criteria affect house prices and the number of housing transactions, then the Help to Buy Scheme has certainly provided it.

When the credit crunch arrived, banks simply did not want to lend. Anything over a 70% loan to value ratio, was considered far too risky. It didn't make sense, because all they did was make less secure the loans they had already made. The effect was to make First Time Buyer properties virtually unsaleable and those sales are what make the rest of the market happen, in volume terms. The immediate result was a drop in house prices and a much less publicised drop in transaction levels from approximately 1.2 million in 2007 to the level of between 500,000 and 600,000 from 2010-2012. The Banks and Building Societies requirement (and they all acted like lemmings), of a 30% deposit, virtually ruled out the first time buyer entering the housing market, without the help of the 'Bank of Mum and Dad'.

Whilst all this has caused great difficulty to members of the public, who needed to move and simply couldn't; those who perhaps inherited a property and had to sell at a vastly reduced figure, the effect on the house building industry was pretty traumatic. Large corporate builders had built so many starter homes that they simply could not sell in any quantity or at a price that would allow them to make a profit. Unlike the general public, they had the power to lobby government and that is precisely what has happened. Since the Help to Buy Scheme, builders share prices have rocketed, and the number of sales of new builds has gone through the roof. Linked to the help for the builders, is a relaxation of planning regulations in and around towns and villages, with building being carried out at such a pace that there is now a shortage of concrete blocks.

The Help to Buy Scheme was first rolled out for new build only. What it did was very simple. It basically restored the public's ability to obtain a 95% mortgage on a new build property only. Houses sell not by what houses offer, but by what the amount the people trying to buy them can afford. The 30% deposit meant that people wanted to buy houses, but simply could not afford to do so. The Government restored that affordability but on new build only. Thus those with a 5% deposit were able to buy new build properties, and during late 2013 and during 2014, Banks and Building Societies reported an increase in mortgage lending. In autumn 2014, a severe drop in mortgage lending was reported, simply because all the new builds had been bought. There was a dam of people wanting to buy, who couldn't, because the credit crunch changed the lending criteria. That change in the lending criteria affected the first timers' ability to buy as they had previously done, and as a result of the Help to Buy Scheme, that ability was restored.

The Help to Buy Scheme has now been extended, or 'rolled out' to the existing housing stock. However, it isn't the same. If you purchase a new build, the Government will provide 20% of the purchase price. If you buy an existing house, the Government will merely guarantee 20% of the asking price. The result of this, is that on a new build, the banks and building societies are saying they are lending 75% loan to value and will give an affordable rate of interest, whereas on existing properties, even though any loss incurred in a forced sale, up to 70% of the value is guaranteed by the Government. They are taking the view that they are lending 95%, which they consider to be high risk and therefore charge a higher rate of interest, well above that which is available for new build and was available before the credit crunch and therefore not affordable by the buying public. The result of this is that whilst the Help to Buy Scheme has allowed the public to buy new build, it has not eased the situation on existing homes at all.

In fact, it has done the exact opposite. Whilst the talk is of increased housing transactions and an increased number of mortgages, it is mainly new build. Whilst historically statistics of housing transactions only took into account existing homes and not new build, there is no doubt that the mortgage numbers and supposed improvement in the housing market, is including new build. The effect on the general housing market and housing transactions for existing homes was generally catastrophic in late 2013 and 2014. The reason is very simple. The Help to Buy Scheme has 'done what the credit crunch did'. It has taken the first time buyer away from the existing house market. Thus, if you take a typical village with 2 – 3 bedroomed terraced houses, prospective first time buyers cannot afford to buy them, because the mortgage finance is not available. If he can afford to buy, he can only afford at a level of say 30% down and the people who own them, who bought prior to the credit crunch, cannot afford to accept that money as they would be in negative equity. The funding that the current owner received is not available to the next purchaser. However, in the same village is a new estate of bright shiny starter homes with many more being built at an alarming rate. Perhaps these may be preferable, but most certainly they are affordable thanks to the Help to Buy Scheme. Hence the current first time buyer generally is buying new build over existing houses, as that is all he can get an affordable mortgage on.

The effect on the general market is that having lost the first time buyer to new build, the person they would have bought from cannot enter the market and do not purchase another property. They are trapped in a small home when naturally they would purchase a larger house, whose owner in turn would purchase another house. First Time Buyers are essential to the general market to give that market mobility. The Scheme, as it has not been offered to the existing home market to the same extent, has taken away those who may have been able to afford an existing home albeit at a lower price than perhaps the original owner paid, but he then could have at least made offers on the next property within the existing housing pool and started the chain process. If you get less for one house, you pay less for the next house and it is the differential of affordability that is important. The chances of improving the existing house market have been substantially reduced by the Help to Buy Scheme, as it has been made far easier

money as soon as they are occupied, because the next purchaser will not be able to afford as much as a good rate Help to Buy Mortgage will not be available to them.

Who has the Help to Buy Scheme helped then? Obviously it has helped the big corporate builders as well as medium sized speculative estate style developers and it has helped the city. It may even help the economy by 'building us out of recession'. In the short term, it has allowed people to purchase a home that would be unavailable to them as a mortgage would simply not have been offered, because of the lending policy and criteria of British Building Societies and Banks. In the short time, these purchasers are most certainly losers in terms of capital value, because their properties will not be able to be sold for the price they paid, as generally the prospective purchaser will not be able to raise the same mortgage. The sale price achieved by the builder will not be achievable in general terms, by the new prospective purchasers.

The losers however are those wishing to move in the general housing market. The reasons for needing to move house are manifold: those who are infirm needing sheltered accommodation, to those needing a smaller house because they are no longer strong enough to maintain their current property, from those needing a larger house because their family has increased, from those needing to move with employment. There are many more reasons. It is these people who are the biggest losers. Ignore prices, it doesn't matter whether housing prices are going up or going down, houses can be sold and it is the differential between prices that is important. If you get more you pay more. In times of inflation, you get more but you pay more. In times of deflation, you get less but you pay less, although it is far more difficult. What the Help to Buy Scheme has done, is taken away the First Time Buyer, the life blood of the established house market and it has done, yet again, what the credit crunch did, in areas away from the south-east where more buyers can raise a deposit, which is virtually make people prisoners in their own homes. It is not a case of dropping prices it is a case of the inability of people to do anything. If you don't have a large deposit, you cannot get started.

It seems to me, that yet again, big business has been favoured at the expense of the British public, who ironically as the tax payers, are providing the money to pay more for a product.

What is happening in our towns and villages, is that older properties are simply not selling; it will soon be the case that you will have many empty 2 – 3 bedroomed traditional starter homes that nobody can sell, but at giveaway prices. This is happening already. More houses are being built in some areas than there is population to fill them. These empty properties will have Council Tax levied on them at 150%.

So who has the Help to Buy Scheme really helped?

Chapter 20

The Battle of The Estate Agents - Online v High Street

I most certainly believe there is a place for On-line Estate Agency, as much as anything because of the misunderstanding of how the market place actually works by the general public, and I certainly believe that the market place these entrepreneurs are entering into is simply not understood by them. It comes down to the old adage of anybody can do Estate Agency, and we can use Estate Agents selling houses as fly paper for selling other products. It very simply is a different angle on the onslaught on Estate Agency by the big institutions in the 1980s.

Any job, profession is evolving all the time, and particularly with the massive change in technology that has taken place. The difficulty is, that technocrats have a problem, in they think that technology can become the major part, instead of the supporting part, of the selling process, just as the corporate onslaught affected the market, so will the on-line attack. It will of course reduce the number of sales available to existing Agents. This will make it more difficult to survive, which you may say is a good thing and fair competition rules, but competition backed by entrepreneurs putting vast amounts of money behind national advertising, without necessarily understanding how the market place works, will simply mean less profitability for those that do. Until the powers that be see that selling houses is not simply a sales situation but also a professional situation, then this will not change.

From the public's perspective, I think they believe that on average ,a properly structured, properly paid for service, will on average bring better results. A difficulty that the Real Estate Agency has always experienced is that, particularly in country properties, let us be kind and say inexperienced competitor, can place a ridiculously high value on a property, as opposed to an asking price and sometimes with unique properties somebody pays it. The whole transaction happens seamlessly in that one instance. Transfer this to an On-line Agency and the individual vendor has sold his property for a high price at a low fee and he is extremely happy. The problem for the market is, whilst there is always the exception and lucky hit, if in general the advice is wrong, as we have shown earlier, the working of the market tends to be affected and transaction levels fall.

The appeal to the vendor of the on-line agent is the low fees, the justification is most people look on-line anyway., and Real Estate Agents don't do any more work for their money.

To try and give a comparison, then we have to assume that both the On-line and High Street Agent gives a good service within their limitations. We then need to look at the different aspects or On-line Agency and the local High Street Agent. We have discussed above that there is always the lucky hit and the exceptional circumstance, and we have to ignore that, and take a graph of probability over a number of instructions and transactions. The first attraction of On-line agents to any vendor are the low fees. On-line Agents claim immediately to have saved hundreds of thousands of pounds of fees for their clients. They omit to say how many fees have been paid up front, without having secured a sale. Bearing in mind, many of these On-line Agencies are just starting, and it is yet to be proven that they can exist off the fee levels that they are charging, so it could be that you pay for a service from an On-line Agent, that then in the future goes out of business because it cannot sustain the level at which the charges it is making. The distortion to the market place as mentioned above is obvious. That is not your problem and you have a situation here and now.

It stands to reason that if an On-line Agent is to provide the same service as a High Street Agent, then given a similar profit margin on each sale, his fees need to cover the services provided by the real High Street Agent less the savings of being on-line only. So what are these savings and indeed are there extra costs? The savings on the average office will be on the following items.

1. No local newspaper advertising.
2. A half/one less receptionist. Bear in mind On-line Agents say no-one calls into high street offices any more.
3. The saving of the high street office rent and rates.
4. Time spent preparing window frontage and cost of displays.

The paper advertising is very much reduced these days, whereas Agents used to advertise every week within the local rag, it is in many cases ever 2 – 4 weeks. It is true that Rightmove charge per office and they will no doubt negotiate a far different deal with On-line Agents but I believe they currently have to pay by region. The fact is that the cost reduction by being an On-line Agent is not that great. They still have to advertise on the portals, they still the staff and the infrastructure, to cope with enquiry, arrange viewings, and possibly have viewers to provide the same service, and still need to inspect the properties, value them, take details, and still have to service it from the time the property is sold subject to contract. One on-line major Agent in 2015 had one local expert, to cover all of North Lancashire and Cumbria. No doubt that will change, but the initial cost of trekking up and down two of the largest counties in England has to be substantial, not to mention ridiculous in its idea that one such expert can possibly cover that area, and be a local expert! If I travel 20 miles from my office I do not consider myself as well versed or knowledgeable in terms of valuation, where that initial advice is so important, not only for the good of the individual vendor, but for the market place as a whole (this is in terms of if this vendor does not sell because his house is overvalued he then does not become a buyer and affects the market). If the 'local expert' undervalues the house then far from saving the Vendor thousands of pounds they have just cost them thousands.

If we assume the average Estate Agency fee in the north of England is say £3,000 then the On-line Estate Agent is saying they can sell the house for around £500 to £1,000 say exclusive of VAT. But the savings are approximately 30% of the fee of the High Street Agent and yet the charge is less than 30% maximum. So how can they provide the same service?

One advantage the On-line Agent has over the real High Street Agent is that in many cases they will ask for a fee up front. In many cases with the High Street Agent if a property is withdrawn or it hasn't sold, through no fault of the Agent necessarily, or indeed perhaps as often happens where the vendor wants the property put on at a high price and then withdraws it when the Agent can't sell it at a price he never said he could achieve. So there is an advantage there, to the Company, but where is the advantage to the vendor? You are paying for a service you haven't yet received, and indeed you are paying a fee. To the High Street Agent you pay a commission, which is an amount of money paid on a percentage of the price received. The Real Estate Agent gets paid for success whereas the On-line Estate Agent is being paid in many cases just for marketing, not all of course and terms vary.

So when deciding on whether to go with an On-line or real High Street Agent you have to look at how the On-line Agent gives the same service at such a low fee and indeed if you have paid him up front, how interested is he going to be in making your sale happen, particularly when he has introduced the purchaser, and the transaction is at solicitor's stage. The real High Street Agent's job does not stop there and will involve possibly speaking to surveyors and damp proof specialists, and even putting solicitors on the right path.

I understand that the low fee may seem highly attractive but it is yet to be proven that overall that you actually get value for money. The on-line agent will argue that most sales come via the internet and this is only going to get greater. However, currently there are still people alive who do not use the internet. There are also people alive who read the local newspaper, not on-line but buy hard copy. Remember, the marketing exercise of selling houses is to let as many people know that the property is for sale as quickly as possible. If the High Street Agent advertises the property in the paper prior to getting it onto Rightmove, then I can assure you he will get enquiries and at the end of the day the internet is merely another medium, but it has the ability to reach worldwide. Then there is the casual purchaser. People are not necessarily looking to move but suddenly see when they are reading the local paper or passing the high street window, see that a property is for sale. They come in and get details. Go down any high street and you will see that usually the most looked in window is the Estate Agent. If you are going to maximise your price you need to inform as many people as quickly as possible. In earlier chapters, we identified placing the property on the market, putting it on the internet, advertising in the local press or press that is considered suitable, emailing potential purchasers who have registered with you either by email or by calling into the office, or that the Agent has picked up when valuing other properties. The name of the game is to get as many people to the property close together, so that you don't need to over price it and it will find its own level within a reasonable period of time making the market work.

The modern way and especially for people covering areas the size of Lancashire and Cumbria will almost certainly be to over price the property. They claim they have the knowledge from Right move and Zoopla evidence but it is not as good as local knowledge. It only takes one mistake and far from saving the client thousands in fees, you have just cost him thousands in the extra sale price that could have been achieved. So the on-line method means that other means of advertising and maximising the sale price are not considered and that one extra person who could have paid more is not found. When selling your maximum asset, should you not look at every means of advertising that you can? At the end of the day the majority of households in regular areas are purchased by locals moving at different stages of their lives. The people moving from Harrow to Durham are not great. There is one major advantage of a High Street Agent which is very much overlooked. We discussed earlier the selling of alternative properties. It is naïve of On-line Agents to claim that High Street Agents are not visited. It is propaganda to justify their cause. Come and sit in any high street office and see how many people actually come in off the street, either to book a valuation or to pick up property details. It is at this point that with people in front of them the High Street Agent can sell alternatives. It is also surprising how many sales are effected on properties that people have dismissed on-line as being not appropriate, but view when put to them by sales staff who know something about the area and the properties they are selling.

As I have stated there are those who will use On-line Agents because of their cheapness and because it suits their own belief. There will be those vendors who feel able to negotiate and carry out viewings, but the dangers seem to me to be:-

1. By adopting the one advertising medium only, you may not attract other potential purchasers, who could have paid more.
2. The cost of being an On-line Agent is perhaps about 30% less than having a traditional High Street presence, yet their fees are far less. This means they will either not be able to provide the same service, or capital will have to be introduced to under-pin it.

They may well be prepared to do this in the short term, but will not be able to do it in the long term.

3. Payment of fees upfront is fraught with potential difficulties.

4. On-line Agencies claim to have 'local experts' and the fact that they are covering huge areas is in itself disingenuous and should raise alarm bells.

The initial asking price and the property valuation is the most fundamentally important part of the whole marketing exercise. This is particularly true where Agents sell to a fixed price and do not operate an 'open offer system'. It is no good being charged a very low fee, when the property is sold for under its value. Of course, valuation techniques of High Street Agents have been discussed and some of these are far from perfect. The reliance of valuers and the general public on on-line valuations is highly dangerous. I personally have seen a property go on the market with an on-line Agent at the on-line valuation of £1.3 million. From our inspection, we believed the value to lie nearer to £750,000.

It should also be remembered that on-line valuations are based very much from the Inland Revenue's quoted sale figures. I have recently seen one property that we sold for £139,000, reported as having been sold for £199,500. Some transactions are reported, on non-open market situations and the price may be lower or higher, depending upon the tax advantage, to the transferor or transferee. In addition, many transactions are simply not reported.

There is no substitute for good local valuation knowledge and it is imperative that any purchaser gets that. The trouble from the Real Estate Agents perspective is that he is being asked to value, but then loses the business to an

On-line Agent. The vendor has taken his valuation and then goes for the cheap fee.

Whilst the On-line Agents argue that the demise of the High Street Agency is nigh due to their lower costs, this ignores the fact that to get market share and presence, achieved by the High Street Agent either by the local paper or by being on the High Street, the On-line Agent has to spend money on TV, radio and every other form of advertising. That is their High Street cost. Without it, will people automatically look towards them? Certainly not in the short term and in the long term only time will tell, but eventually the online agent will realise that they cannot continue to charge low fees and provide the service. The reason, very simply, is that Estate Agents do not make masses of money. Out of London profitability probably lies between 10% and maximum 20% of gross turnover. The cost savings by being online only are not enough, and advertising to keep market share may well prove more expensive than the high street presence. The on-line business model for me, simply does not stack up.

What it is unfolding though is a huge experiment funded by business people and the City, into how the British public buy and sell what we are continually told is their most important asset, their house.

I believe yet again the welfare of the house owning public is being put at risk. The risk is upfront costs for generally poor service and possibly payment for no result. Poor advice regarding valuation with the danger of under selling and over pricing which then acts to the detriment of the market generally. Much of the above, however exists with the current general estate agency situation, unless you are careful who you choose.

It may be the hope of the investors and entrepreneurs that the house for sale are used yet again to act as fly paper to attract traffic to a site to sell other services. I can see that helping thing to work. In fact, it is the only way I can see it working. On-line agents that have never turned in a profit are suddenly worth millions on the stock exchange, will they justify the faith of investors.?

In an article of 2008 April in the Negotiator it was asked whether agents could migrate from advertising from press to on-line only. Would online agents make it big. Private investor group Hotbed was mentioned backing WOW Property to the tune of £1.65 million. Then there was Bright Sale founded in 2007 and issued a report foreseeing the decline of High Street Estate Agency, forecasting they will be niche status by 2013. Well that has not happened and I am not sure where they are now.

Current new players appear to be much more highly powered. However, the role of an Estate Agent is more than just sales, and it will be interesting to see whether on-line agents can properly service the needs of the house moving public at the fee levels they are trying to charge.

More likely they will hinder the chance of a smooth running property market. Remember good agents make the market run more smoothly.

Chapter 21

The Way Forward

AGENTS & MORTGAGE BROKERING

The Real Estate Agent is not a Mortgage Broker. He believes the interference of that nice financial services world into his world of estate agency, has been a disaster and continues to have an adverse effect on the sale of houses and the workings of the market but also is a conflict of interest, that is not in the best interests of the general public. Some Estate Agents who broke mortgages will deliberately overvalue, just to get contact from the would-be seller. They then try to make money by inspecting the new clients' financial situation and make money from the new client, perhaps by broking new life insurance policies, without even having the instruction to sell his house.

The corporate estate agents are there to sell financial products and some may well be unprofitable were they not able to do so. In February 2016 it was reported 'Countrywide profits plunge 37%' and that 'There was a decline in estate agency and lettings profitability' The new chief executive was quoted as saying 'However, the importance of the breadth of our portfolio through such a diversified business as ours was underlined by the market beating performance delivered in financial services, commercial and surveying.' You could read that as saying the estate agency section is being propped up by the other sections, but we need to do it to get financial services leads and for our profile. Look at any corporate year-end figures and the profitability for estate agency in relation to total outlay, does not compare with their other activities and particularly since the credit crunch, with low transaction levels would have been unsustainable. Do they know something we do not?

Local Building Societies, who do not care if they make profit from Estate Agency as long as they get financial leads, would certainly leave if they could not sell mortgages to their purchasers. This would leave Estate Agency open to people who actually just want to sell property and be paid accordingly by their client the vendor.

Many people will point out the advantage of knowing that the purchaser can afford to buy the property, but there are other ways of finding that out. Should the buyer have to reveal how much he can afford?

Currently, we are stuck with the situation, where the Real Estate Agent who does not sell mortgages, is competing against people who can afford to lessen fees because they are making money out of the purchaser. Some may see this as a good thing, but generally the conflict of interest situation costs the client, who is supposed to be the Vendor not the purchaser.

ACTION 1: Ban the sale of mortgages by Estate Agents.

OVER VALUATION

The sale and purchase of a house is, we are reliably told, in the vast majority of cases, the largest single transaction that most people make in their lives. It seems strange to me that the people who carry out this transaction and offer advice on it, do not need to have any professional qualification whatsoever, or at least some proof of competency. Anyone can set up as an Estate Agent. The Real Estate Agent knows that in a busy office, there is hardly a day goes by that he is not required to make a decision or give advice based on planning law, contract law, or property law. Hardly a day goes by when some issue brought up by a survey, needs to be discussed with a client and a decision made as to how serious the structural problem identified is and if it should impact on the price. A head of a large corporate estate agency, reflecting upon their success, was reported as saying that the business quickly grew, 'because we were up against Chartered Surveyors and we were full of sales'. Was it suddenly that Chartered Surveyors were no longer able to do the work? I will leave you to draw your own conclusions and what was meant by 'sales'.

A few years ago, there was a clamour to license Estate Agents but the powers that be did not want to do that; the main reason being that small companies which have been trading quite successfully, will suddenly have respectability. They would be able to say that they were under a government scheme and they are part of it. We couldn't have all those nice little individual companies able to say they are a Licensed Estate Agent. All those little companies that need controlling individually: Estate Agency, by and large is a cottage industry, full of small companies with caring bosses, who try to do the job to the best of their ability and in the main, give good customer care. As the size of a company increases, and the distance of those making the decisions with regard to how the business is run gets larger, customer care falls at an alarming rate, and it becomes about targets, market share and board count.

As far as the 'powers that be' think, the best way to regulate Estate Agency is to have it overseen by a few corporate companies with good public relations departments, that can blether on about how they 1) train their staff, 2) are members of every Ombudsman Scheme, 3) have every complaints procedure in place.

The true intention is of course to take something that is essentially a local activity requiring local knowledge and customise it so as to direct as much of the revenue created by the activity to themselves and their Corporate masters in the City.

If a young man or woman wanted to start an Estate Agency today and be their own boss, where is the incentive? There are very few people coming into the profession and one of the main reasons for this is that they do not want to work for banks and large corporate companies. The type of individual coming into the profession or job is changing and the person about to be employed expects to stay employed with little expectation of being self-employed and running the business to his own moral compass. Of course, there are opportunities of advancement, but to achieve these he will have to tow the corporate business line.

The powers that be are happy for someone who comes from 200 miles away, to be employed and within his first day, be able to go out and value properties within a new area. Respectability is given to his 'opinion' by the fact that he is employed by a large company and therefore, the implication is that the advice must be right. Of course, they don't value. They probably know within 20% what the value is, but then hike it up to be on the safe side. Some Agencies cynically and consistently over value to get market share. Will this situation change? It could do. Without restricting entry to Estate Agency, then the biggest chance of exercising some control is at the point of valuation. I believe that if you are carrying out market appraisals for any company, then you should have to place a Valuation on a property not just a suggested Asking Price and you should have to register your valuations with a government controlled body . In the modern world of computers, this is ridiculously easy to do. The Inland Revenue, for some years now, has published the prices achieved of all house sales. It has done no good for the Real Estate Agents blood pressure, as he sees what the houses, that he valued previously, achieved - usually about what he said or less. He was right, but did not get the business. So called 'valuers' are getting away with what is tantamount to giving at best negligent advice and at worst, fraudulent, over and over again. The irony is that these Agents are hindering and reducing their own local market.

When a valuer carries out a valuation or market appraisal, it should be stated as a valuation; the Agent then recommends an asking price. When the property is sold, you have to input the selling price. If over a period of a year, there is more than a 15% differential between valuation and achieved sale price, you are investigated. If it continues, without there being proper reasons, you are barred from valuing for 6 months and then have to re-apply, having worked within your Agency on sales. Simple. Taking valuations over the period of a year, would allow for the odd 'lucky hit' - anomalies that can happen.

The Real Estate Agent follows other valuers who have sometimes been in a property for a maximum of five minutes. Given a figure without notes and given a figure without any reference to other properties. Is that what the public deserves? Valuers having to register their valuation would make all companies far more attentive to this most important professional job, and it would increase transactions throughout the country, because the valuations would be correct and the properties marketed at the correct asking price (subject of course, to their clients' approval and instructions) and they would sell far more quickly which would in turn encourage more people to move house. The Real Estate Agent supports such an overseeing body because it will have a practical purpose and effect.

ACTION 2: Registration of all Valuations for Sale Purposes with consequences if errant.

SURVEYORS AND MORTGAGING VALUATIONS

Some years ago, many Chartered Surveyors decided that they did not want to follow people around, doing Estate Agency valuations, being right but not getting the business and their integrity would not let them over value to maintain market share, and very simply, they could get paid more money by doing professional work. Up against the 'new brand of sales', many retreated to the professional work of surveying and valuing, rating, development work and of course, commercial estate agency, which was of little interest to the institutions. This is a great shame. Even if the doctrines were split within the office, with different people doing different functions, the fact was that within that office there was an awful lot more information. Not only could the surveyors see what the estate agents were selling and what they were selling the properties for, but the estate agents from the surveyors, had details of what they were valuing, how big they were and how much they made. In other words, there was more comparable evidence for the individual.

When Surveyors split from Estate Agents, they also lost touch with the market. They lost touch with the immediacy of impact of something happening within the locality and the effect that was having on prices. It would come through eventually, but they would not see it as quickly and this, coupled with the fact that the transaction levels have dropped so dramatically, means that many surveyors have far less comparable evidence and therefore knowledge on which to place accurate valuations.

Nevertheless, that it happened is understandable and for a while, surveying practices were employed by the major banks and building societies, but gradually, this work began to reduce. The banks and building societies realised that there was money in this. Fees that the public were charged, in addition to the Valuation for Mortgage Purposes, could include Home Buyer Reports and Full Structural Surveys and so, the banks employed Chartered

Surveyors and began to set up their own surveying companies.

Colleys Professional Services was owned originally by the Halifax Building Society. Connells Professional Services is owned by the Skipton. E-serve is a sister company of Reeds Rains and Your Move which is owned by a parent company of LSL Solutions. They in turn are owned by Venture Capitalists etc. Countrywide Surveyors is part of the old Hambro Group, which again is owned by Venture Capitalists. Briefly, what happens is that when your mortgage application goes forward, once it has been approved in principle and sent up for a survey, it is panelled out, by and large, to these major groups. Local building societies may have their own in-house surveyors, or sometimes contract local surveyors, but by and large, a mortgage valuation is panelled out to the Corporate Surveyors. It is possible for a Purchaser to buy from a Building Society Estate Agents, get a mortgage from the same Society and have the valuation carried out by a Surveyor employed by the Society through its sister company. The same banks used to insist on independent surveyors signing a form to say they had no known conflict of interest, but such a thing was conveniently forgotten once the banks employed their own surveyors. The purchaser thinks he is getting an independent valuation! Surely, this is testament to the fact that building society/bank valuations are for the security of the building society and not to advise the person purchasing the property. You are certainly not getting an independent valuation and I would suggest Valuations are more often than not placed at sale price, as long as the Banks loan is secure, as directed by Banks to the surveyors. So purchasers can be paying too much without being told.

What is worse, in an effort to cut costs, there are few regional offices and surveyors cover huge areas. It is not unusual for surveyors to travel 100 miles to carry out a valuation. To get comparable evidence, they troll the Estate Agents offices taking sales particulars of similar properties at vastly differing prices, and even have the brass neck to ask local surveyors! On many occasions, they come and ask The Real Estate Agent for information. In one recent case, I was about to ring a Probate Department to ask them if they would consider moving Agent, since we had valued a particular property at £380,000 to £400,000 and it was placed on the market with a competitor at £550,000. I was greeted by a smiling Chartered Surveyor who I knew from many years ago, who had driven some 100 miles and had looked at the property. I had the valuation and all the information in my hand. 'You were right he said, it was sold for £381,000'. The last time I had seen the price reduced was to £495,000. I told him to flick the page over and there was a list of comparable evidence of bungalows. 'Oh great do you mind if I write these down, thanks very much, see you in another 20 years'.

Local knowledge is paramount in valuation and so again, the valuation and valuation expertise has been dumbed down and as long as the bank's money is secure, that is all they are interested in. That they charge the prospective mortgagor for this does need changing. If the banks want their own valuation to make sure their money is secure, then very simply they should pay for it. This would mean that money is available for people to take local advice if they require valuation advice and survey advice. The conflict of interest is yet again absolutely clear.

Short term gain was why this happened, but short term never works in the long term. It seems a jolly good wheeze to have valuers haring up and down the country, packing in as many valuations as their masters can give them, often at the cost of professional accuracy, but the banks will soon run into a little problem. The staff are ageing. The Real Estate Agent did not become a Chartered Surveyor, to be employed by a bank. I had a belief in my own ability and wanted to work for myself. The modern Surveyor, is being denied that possibility, or at least probability and so again, the aspirations of the individual coming into the profession are changing and the numbers are dropping. The average age of chartered surveyors is now 55 years, we are struggling to fit through the creep holes and teeter from joist to joist. Soon, there will not be enough Surveyors to do the banks bidding. Big business it is though. Of one large corporate Estate Agency in September 2007 it was reported 'profits from surveying during the first half of 2007 were £11.7m against £9.8m a year earlier and nearly double the profits from estate agency and financial services.' That was before the credit crunch and the collapse of estate agency revenues. The surveying section was making more than the estate agency section then, this for a very much smaller infrastructure and cost.

Interestingly, when the corporate surveyors get too busy, they then try and engage the local Chartered Surveyors, but only give them half a fee or in some cases one third of the normal fee for doing the work. At that rate, it is hardly worth carrying out the work and so the local Chartered Surveyor is struggling to command the fee income, at a reasonable level for time taken. If the country wants Surveyors, then very simply this needs to change. If the banks do not want the trouble of dealing with individual surveyors, it is perhaps understandable. It can be panelled just as they are doing, but these are Panel Managers and instruct either corporate or private surveyors, whichever is the most appropriate, who must demonstrate proper local knowledge. That being a reasonable way forward would allow private Chartered Surveyors in localities far from corporate surveying centres, to flourish, provide a proper service and above all, give the prospective purchaser the service and professional integrity that he deserves, or indeed just the informed valuation that he deserves.

The crowning irony facing all surveyors is that we are liable to sued by lenders as they are selling repossessed properties due to the credit crunch at figures below the valuation price paid, but it is the banks themselves that are causing the drop in values by restricting lending and reducing the publics affordability.

ACTION 3:

a) Banks pay for their own mortgage valuations. They can instruct their own Surveyors but they must instruct Surveyors who work within a 30-mile radius of the subject property.

b) Private Reports, House Buyers and Surveys cannot be appointed by the Building Society, but must be arranged by the Purchaser if he requires one.

THE MORTGAGE LENDING MULTIPLE

The Real Estate Agent remembers the days when there was a large number of small to medium sized Building Societies. The Building Societies that have stuck to their mutual basis have worked on the understanding that they borrow money in, or take deposits, pay out at a certain interest level, pay interest at a certain level to those parties and lend the same money out at a higher rate of interest, continue to prosper. It isn't rocket science and those that have stuck to the principal, survive. The truth is that main stream banks are no doubt in the mortgage business for the long term and since they have taken over, it is probably very necessary that they are.

However, there has to be a realisation, that housing is a social issue. It cannot be treated totally as a money-making exercise, without causing great hardship and the lowering of general living standards and happiness. This is a very crowded island and many people do not have lovely places to live in terms of the actual environment and the one thing they need, is to be able to go home. We don't have fantastic weather and the one thing we need, is that when we go home into that little warm cocoon, it is reasonable and affordable. Increasing the amount of the multiple of salary for what a person can borrow, caused too great a hike in inflation and has meant that we all live in homes, for which we are paying higher mortgage payments and, more importantly, a far higher proportion of our wages, than had the banks not increased that multiple. They did this in an effort to lend and make more money and originally increase their share of the mortgage market. They have made the cost of UK housing the highest in the world.

The way forward, is that it must never happen again. The banks make a good and easy profit from mortgage lending; it is easy money and providing they do not alter the lending criteria, it is safe. I do not think you could ever be entirely rigid on the multiples issue, but if it does rise again, it must be for social reasons and not for more profit. Interest rates are at a record low and if they were to rise, it could well affect people's affordability. Perhaps we now have a greater understanding of the consequences of increasing the multiple, and there needs to be greater cooperation and understanding between governments and banks, on the housing issue and their direction to the banks and their moral responsibilities.

ACTION 4: The multiple of income to loan ratio needs fixing and cannot be altered by any lender.

AUTHOR'S NOTE: Since this was written the Governor of the Bank of England has restricted the multiple to 4.5 times on 85% of a banks residential mortgage portfolio.

THE BUY TO LET MORTGAGE

It may have been as a response to the then labour governments' desire to have more private rented property available in the UK, but more likely it was the rapacious nature of the banks that led to them introducing the Buy to Let Mortgage. Effectively a commercial mortgage, it meant they could charge a higher rate of interest, achieve a higher degree of security with a 70% loan to ratio value and charge higher arrangement fees: all this, in the relative security of the residential housing market in the UK. In my view, it has been a complete disaster. I have no issue at all with those people who used the Buy to Let Mortgage as a means of acquiring property to let. Some have dabbled, some have built up property empires and good luck to them. The opportunity was given; why not take advantage of it? With other forms of investments and pensions showing such a poor return, Buy to Let offers a relatively secure investment, with a reasonable return. In the early days, it also provided good capital growth of the asset. The immediate effect however, was to price many first time buyers out of the market. As first time buyers as normal tried to buy a house, they found it went beyond their affordability and was purchased by a Buy to Let Landlord. They then had no choice but to rent property, paying rent that probably exceeded the mortgage payment they would have had to pay on the same property. For the overall good of the housing market and mobility in the country, you need the first time buyer coming in and moving later. The change in lending criteria by the banks has had a tremendously adverse effect on the ability of the first time buyer to get on the rung. Even had they maintained the 95% mortgage, the higher rents having to be paid as opposed to mortgage payments, by the aspiring householder, means that it takes them longer to save for a deposit. The properties that are then occupied as rental properties become a long term investment, rather than a stepping stone to something better. The inability of many would-be purchasers to get onto the housing ladder means that the process falters when say a house of the 3-bedroom family type, can prove more difficult to sell. First time buyers are now buying the normal second step property, but it takes them longer to achieve it for the reasons given above and the strength and fluidity of the housing market is diminished. Basically, if the Buy to Let mortgage had not been made available, most of these houses would have been purchased by first time buyers and the market would have worked in a more normal way, at least until the Credit Crunch, when the banks changed the criteria to wanting a 30% deposit; even for the first time buyer.

The success of the private landlord has been noted by the banks and institutions and it was mooted in 2014 that the institutions were stating that they had an interest in being allowed in purchasing residential investments. It seems what the corporates and institutions want, they get and whether this is the reason for the Chancellor in late 2015 changing the goal posts for private landlords in relation to tax relief and mortgage repayments and the surcharge of 3% stamp duty on anything but private homes, except of course for the institutions, we will probably never know. To make these changes to people who have planned for a certain situation is in my view outrageous. Those who have acquired these properties under a certain situation and tax regime, should be able to continue but overall, I believe the Buy to Let mortgage has been a disaster for the general housing market and the welfare of the would-be house owning public. If people want to invest their own money into residential properties then they should be allowed to do so, but they should not be able to borrow money from banks to do so. Up until the Chancellors announcement, the amount of lending for the Buy to Let market was increasing dramatically. The Buy to Let Mortgage should be banned. They should be removed from the market place but in conjunction the banks must be made to stop their unnecessary demand for a 20% deposit and take up and give reasonable rates for a 95% mortgage which will allow first time buyers to purchase houses more easily other than new build. The Help to Buy Scheme has proven that people can afford 95% if the rates are reasonable. Therefore, there may be a slight adjustment downwards to prices throughout a chain of property sales, but it would allow many first time buyers currently renting, to get onto the market and in a short time the housing market itself would get greater stability and fluidity.

of housing transactions throughout the country and the mobility of the public. The Banks have not realised that by doing this, they are making less secure the money they have already lent for home purchase, by effectively diminishing the market.

What difference does it make to the banks, if they allow people to move house as at the same level. Intervention is again required by the Bank of England, to force the banks to comply with a request to port a mortgage at the same rate of interest that is currently being paid by the borrower.

ACTION: Banks have to allow people to port their mortgage at the same rate as they are paying now on Tracker Mortgages.

ANOTHER FORM OF MORTGAGE PROVIDER

The Help to Buy Scheme is the most recent evidence of how changing lending criteria boosts housing market transactions and prices. It shows that First Time Buyers can and want to buy property, if they are given the chance of a 95% mortgage, but a requirement for a 30% or even 20% deposit, effectively stops them buying. Housing is important for the general well-being of the British people and consideration needs to be given to this by the Institutions and not just their own ability to make a profit.

From the mid-'80s until deregulation, the vast majority of lending was carried out by Building Societies, who were mutual and there for the good of their lenders. Regulations

Housing & Construction 1980-1990
Bank of England 1991 Onwards

Table 40 **Numbers of mortgage advances per year in Great Britain**
Thousands

	1980	1985	1990	1991	1992	1993	1994	1995	1996	1997	1998	1999	2000	2001	2002	2003
Building societies	675	1,073	780	661	531	561	602	513	589	396	230	304	311	225	247	197
+ Banks		176	333	316	327	397	359	346	431	674	678	757	734	965	1,061	967
+ Insurance companies	18	19	26													
+ Local authorities	16	23	8													
+ Other specialist lenders				83	38	34	52	50	65	116	127	82	68	68	113	202
= Total	709	1,291	1,147	1,060	896	992	1,013	909	1,085	1,186	1,035	1,143	1,113	1,257	1,422	1,365

Sources: Housing and Construction Statistics (annual volumes) for 1980 to 1990; Bank of England 1991 onwards.
Notes: The 1980 figures are for England and Wales only and exclude council house sales. Thereafter, figures are for Great Britain, and include council house sales. Abbey National Plc figures included with the banks figures from July 1989. The 1980 figures also reflect the continuing trend for building societies to convert to banks. The figures for banks and other specialist lenders for the years 1991 to 1997 are understood to include The Bank of England data from 1991 onwards also reflects the continuing trend for building societies to convert to banks. The figures for banks and other specialist lenders for the years 1991 to 1997 are understood to include remortgage advances as well as loans for house purchase. From 1998 the data relates solely to advances for house purchase.

Over the years they have acted mainly in their own interest, rather than for the good of the British public: in many spheres, but no more than in housing. By increasing the multiples of income with the ability to lend from 2.5% to as much as 4.5% in the late '80s, they caused massive inflation, which meant that people had to pay more to buy the same house. When interest rates rose, they reduced the multiple, meaning that the same type of individual on the same income could not borrow the same amount of money and therefore could not pay what the previous purchaser had paid. The Banks created negative equity overnight and again, ironically, made what they had already lent on, less secure.

They were to do exactly the same in 2002/2003 and then came the credit crunch. I hear people say that the British public borrow too much and they brought it on themselves. I cannot see this argument; there were no particular repossessions or difficulties until the credit crunch. It was the Banks messing up affairs in other spheres that then caused financial difficulties within the economy, which in turn impacted upon people's ability to pay their mortgages.

The requirement of a 30% deposit presumably is seen by the banks as a means of ensuring adequate security for when they lend on the next property. What it in fact did, was kill the market completely as First Time Buyers cannot get onto the housing ladder and it is they who primarily keep the housing market moving. The banks increase of multiples was described as 'lending without conscience'. This is a withdrawal of funding without conscience, and as it makes what they have already lent on less secure, by reducing prices, it means that it is also pretty witless, as the saying 'safe as houses' was not thought up for nothing. The banks could not have a safer and secure way of making money and yet they have embarked upon an all or nothing policy. They have upped the multiples of income to loan, the public have had to pay higher prices, with an increased amount of their income being spent on a property that they could have bought for less money, had that increase of multiple not been given. The withdrawal of high percentage mortgages has made it impossible for people to sell and in turn buy other property. People have literally been imprisoned in their own homes. Even at huge discounts, property can be unsaleable, particularly in country areas. Widows with large houses are unable to move to town bungalows and live their lives in a comfortable and controlled fashion: just one example of the type of situation which the banks latest policy has caused, to the detriment of the public.

Completed Rates – 'HMRC Negotiator' – April 2008

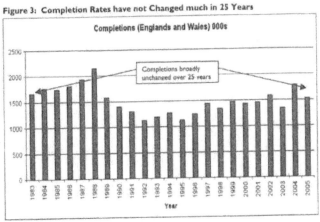

Figure 3: Completion Rates have not Changed much in 25 Years

Source: HMRC

197

The table shows total property transactions from 1983 to 2005. It comments that they are broadly unchanged. We have discussed the reasons for this, despite the huge number of houses built since 1983. The table includes commercial sales which historically accounted for approximately 10%. Residential sales peaked in 2006 at say 1.4m and after the introduction of a 30% deposit requirement dropped to circa 600,000 in 2010 which presumably included many repossessions sold at literally knock down prices at public auctions.

To me, it is clear that high street commercial banks cannot be trusted with lending money for house purchase. The Bank of England's decision to limit the multiple is to be welcomed, but far more is necessary to allow the First Time Buyer to buy, other than new build, and to make sure that those in lending do so in a responsible fashion as the banks are refusing to lend at reasonable rates, other than where there is a high deposit. Other players will and undoubtedly are trying to come into the market. Regulation is required but not over regulation. It really is simple. Fix the multiple, (as has been done), fix the amount and give a band between what the banks can borrow in at and what they can lend out at. Does it really need to be more complicated? Is it really that much different from what happened when Building Societies had the monopoly of lending for house purchase, before deregulation and Big Bang?

It may be that a central mortgage bank, with the ability to borrow money and lend for housing purposes only, is the answer. It really is not rocket science and mutual Building Societies worked very well for many years, until deregulation.

Whatever happens, currently there is a complete impasse; the banks are refusing to lend unless the government gives 20%, or guarantees 20%. The guarantee of course is on existing buildings, not new build and as it is only a guarantee, the banks are saying they are lending 95% and therefore the rate is so punitive that few take it up. The general requirement of a 20% deposit by the banks is holding back the market in terms of transactions. It is unclear how this situation will change, without radical action.

Unless of course there is another motive!

As long as any new body/lender/institution does not alter dramatically the lending criteria, then you will not have huge house inflation or deflation. Inflation may happen in wealthier areas where people can save money more easily and thus put in a bigger deposit, but this is natural. It simply means that property prices increase in prosperous areas, because people are earning good money rather than the banks increasing the amount they lend. There have been many examples of Bank's behaviour resulting in loss to their clients/customers. Isn't this the worst: changing lending criteria to suit their own circumstances? They have cost the British public huge amounts of money by making them pay more for the same commodity or by making them lose money on it. Their actions have meant that people are unable to move and get on with life. Yet all this appears to be accepted, as though it is some natural consequence in the market. It is not! As the Help to Buy Scheme proved the desire to buy is there if the availability of funding is there. It has taken a Government scheme to prove it is the change of lending criteria which affects the market. In my view this is a scandal, that has been directly felt by so many people in dramatic and tragic ways.

Where are the Estate Agents in all this? The Real Estate Agent knows that in times of inflation you get more, but you pay more. He knows that in times of deflation you get less but you pay less. The second situation is far harder; it is required to link sales together. The Real Estate Agent encourages people to look before they have sold as they do not know what they can afford to accept, unless they know the price at which they can buy. It is about linking sales together. The majority of Estate Agents still tell people not to look until they have sold and still over value to keep market share. This results in others, who are thinking of moving, looking at the market and thinking it is so poor that there is no point putting their houses on the market. Suddenly we are being told that there is a shortage of houses coming to the market. A lot of people think that if it is going to take months or years to sell their house, there is little point. The combination of Bank's lending policies and lack of integrity on valuation and sheer lack of expertise in Estate Agency has meant a huge drop in housing transactions and a lack of mobility for the general public. If in 1988 there were 2 million transactions in England and Wales, with a huge number of houses having been built since that time, common sense says it should be at least 2.5million to 3million today and yet it is hovering at about the 800 to 900,000 mark.

ACTION A properly regulated, controlled institution, perhaps a national bank for mortgage lending is required.

Chapter 22

The Great Conspiracy Theory

There will be those who think this book is fantasy and there will be those who will shortly think I have gone completely into the realms of fantasy. So I will start it thus.

Once upon a time bankers were bankers. They had integrity and by their lending and investment activities, they wanted to give investors a fair return, safeguard their deposits, make a reasonable and sensible profit by lending to whom they thought had a reasonable business venture or proposition and who would be above to re-pay the interest and eventually the capital they lent to them. More recently, they have begun to lend to those seeking to purchase a house, at a rate that allowed themselves to make a reasonable profit.

Banks suddenly realised that the activities that their borrowers went into in some cases could be undertaken by themselves. Why let other people make profits when bankers could make profits out of doing the business that their clients were doing just as easily. Suddenly, if you delved, you found that the Insurance Company that you were dealing with was in fact a sub company of some high street bank. I am sure there will be many other industries that are involved, that I do not know about but let's deal with those that have affected the housing market and directly or indirectly the Real Estate Agent.

MORTGAGE BROKERS & INDEPENDENT FINANCIAL ADVISORS

Independent financial advisors were precisely that, either completely individual or part of small individual companies. Independent financial advisers deal with other matters apart from advising on mortgages. Indeed, many independent financial advisors do not deal with mortgages at all, but some do. Primarily they deal with investments which are usually linked in some way to investment, managed through banks and insurance companies: they deal with pension funds and they advise on the risk factor of the various investments into which people could put their money, which usually gave a better return and more capital growth than simply investing money in a bank or building society.

On a lighter side, it always seems to me that the banks and building societies and the corporate estate agent has missed a trick here. Whilst they saw a link with regard to selling mortgages, they seem largely to have missed the link with regard to the investment market. Hey Corporates you read it here first. The Real Estate Agent is aware of many investment opportunities; people are selling houses for many different reasons. It may be a holiday home but they don't use it anymore because they no longer feel comfortable driving the long distance because of age. It is completely paid for. What will they do with the money?

It may be you are selling a bungalow in a probate situation where you are selling the property for the beneficiaries. What will they do with the money? Maybe somebody is down-sizing from a big house to a smaller bungalow, what will they do with the capital left over? I may be wrong but I don't know of many corporate estate agents that have links to any independent financial advisors, or at least use this type of lead.

Independent Mortgage Advisors were often mortgage brokers, but there were many mortgage brokers who were not independent financial advisors, they simply brokered mortgages. Whether by accident or design, in a so called effort to clean up the industry, the numbers of them have diminished dramatically. Ah I can hear you say! They needed cleaning out! What about selling all those endowment policies? The endowment policy was a good product. You simply paid money to an insurance company which invested the money with which you would have repaid capital. You simply pay the interest on the loan. With a capital re-payment mortgage, at the beginning of the term, for some reason which I have never understood, you hardly pay back any capital, it is nearly all interest. Remember in those days of yore, people moved every 7 years, so effectively, you were paying a fixed amount through the bank for 20 years, but if you moved after 7 years, you had hardly paid any capital back at all, you then moved house because of your family needs and you started with another 25-year term with practically the same amount owing. Good business for the banks. The endowment policy meant that you were consistently repaying the capital from day one; if you moved after 7 years you had repaid some of the capital effectively through the endowment policy. At the end of the term, your capital was paid off by the investment you had made with the insurance company. The problem was not with the product; it was with the people who invested the money. They either got it wrong or took too high a management charge out of the fund so that when the term was finished, there was not enough money in the policy to pay back all the capital. Did independent mortgage brokers know about this when they sold the product? I don't think so - they were talking about 20 years hence. The problem was with the institutions who managed the funds.

Nevertheless, under the guise of the Financial Services Authority, the clean-up started and the effect was that many independent financial advisers and mortgage brokers simply gave up. Compliance was the nature of the game and only those with the money to afford compliance departments and the time to carry out compliance (which was probably so complicated that nobody understood it anyway) could survive. The effect of this of course was that the independent financial advisors who had been competition with the bank for the work disappeared, and everybody could then go direct to the banks.

The whole raft of independent professionals was got rid of in the name of compliance, consumer protection and that old mad idea, that the big company will look after the welfare of the public.

Am I suggesting legislation and compliance procedures were in some way tilted towards favouring the banks carrying out most of the work and that therefore there was a way of managing and overseeing the compliance procedures far more easily because there were fewer people were to oversee? Please draw your own conclusions. There was of course the other effect that less broker fees were paid by the Banks and Institutions and as they saw the potential clients direct could sell all those nice financial products, often, that the client did not need.

The effect was to reduce independent professionals, more work was carried out by the banks who then simply sold the British public such products as PPI and they have been paying for mis-selling various products ever since.

SURVEYORS AND MORTGAGE VALUATIONS

We have already discussed at length how banks and building societies created their own surveying companies and then directed valuation work from the mortgage applications that came in, to their own companies. No legislation was needed to do this, when the request to lend money came to them they simply placed the valuation work with their own companies or to panels, who then distributed valuations as far as possible to the Corporate Surveyor. This was irrespective of whether the valuers who worked for them worked in the area where the valuation was to take place or were best place in terms of valuation expertise to carry out the work. It was, is a cartel; they take work from local surveyors because they offer to do a valuation for the mortgage but also carry out a home buyer or structural survey report at a discounted rate. Valuation is dependent on local knowledge; there is no way that valuers from outside of the area can carry it out as well. Whilst in some cases they do have local offices, in many they do not, but it does not matter they will do it anyway. I have seen Surveyors regularly travelling 60 – 100 miles and as far as 150 miles to carry out one valuation. They then have the gall to ask local surveyors and valuers for valuation information, or they collect sales details from local Estate Agents, thereby committing details, not sales prices as comparable evidence.

As with mortgage brokers, the effect is pretty well the same on residential surveyors; they are a disappearing race, Surveyors are getting older, with fewer people entering the profession.

THE HOME INFORMATION PACK

From day one, the Home Information Pack was never about increasing the speed of the housing transaction. Remember, the art of selling houses, is not selling one at a time but putting chains together, moving people from house to house and so involves a chain of say three houses. House A has an information pack, the estate agent could have got the details and got it on to the market in say a week, but remember originally there had to be a home condition report. Questions regarding the legal status of the property had to be researched. Even without the legal part, to get a home buyers report many properties would take three to four weeks, where on earth did they think all the Surveyors were going to come from? It would have taken years, even for the corporates to have trained enough people, so that a survey could be carried out on every house marketed.

The idea originally was you had to have this report prior to marketing. House A has its report and the owner of house B wishes to put an offer in, his offer is acceptable in principle but he has a house to sell and we have to get it on the market . . . Hello . . . we cannot market for another month, so another month goes by and we get to sell in principle to a person who owns property C which is a first time buyer type property. The offer from the owner of property C is accepted on property B. However, we need before we can market, a Home Information Pack involving a whole condition report and answers to the legal status, another month goes by.

We have managed to increase the marketing time of all properties by approximately a month, giving a further three to four months, and extending the chain process by two and a half to three months before we have even started the legal processes. It never ever was about reducing the time period. It was about two things:-

1 You're a Banker and your bank owns corporate surveying companies. You have just invented them. By how much are you going to increase your company's income if every single house that goes on to the market in the country has to have a condition report.

2 The main reason that home buyer reports were introduced was to transfer the conveyancing work that for centuries has been carried out by independent local solicitors. In a run up to the introduction of the whole Home Information Pack, million and millions of pounds was spent setting up companies that would supply the Packs. These were large organisations. Vast infrastructure was created. Hard pressed solicitors were canvassed and invited to give the work to these companies that would provide them with the necessary report with guaranteed turn around time. Not surprisingly, organisations such as HIP HAG (it does not matter what it stood for) were suddenly created, to give some form of spokesperson a platform and the respectability of a body representing

these Pack providers. These impressive authoritative spokesmen, all came from the corporate industry; many came from banks' mortgage departments, others from corporate estate agency. One high profile individual, kept telling the sceptical professionals what a brilliant idea it was, had a quote when googled and his claim to fame seemed to be the following statement 'To me the most re-engineering you need to do is of mind-sets, then people will change the process appropriately, to meet the customer imperative, whether it is a big or small change'. His job as spokesperson was to basically keep telling everybody what a wonderful idea this was.

There seems to be a real growth industry in this sort of thing; it's basically about taking something that is wrong and presenting it with all respectability. Thus someone like Gillian Knight, was given the difficult job of being the Bankers Association spokesman, putting the banks perspective during the credit crunch. I actually felt sorry for her.

The Home Information Pack was not about the subject matter in the report which quite honestly in many cases was pretty useless. It would mention that there was a right over some land but it didn't say where or what. The Real Estate Agent in his solicitor's questions had been establishing this for over 25 years and getting far more information and getting it whilst the marketing was being carried out, so that it was to hand when people started asking the questions. It was not about speeding the process; it was about up-front cost. If you introduce up-front cost, it is a marketing opportunity. Within weeks of the Home Information Pack being required, all of a sudden, free HIPs were being advertised, but to get the free HIP the conveyancing had to be carried out by the licensed conveyancing company which mysteriously but not amazingly, had suddenly appeared behind the HIP provider. Suddenly, Simply HIP had a sister company Simply Conveyancing.

Whilst many people in the wealthier areas would probably have stayed with their trusted solicitor, those in the larger urban conurbations, which is where the corporates make their money, would not. It would have been a free for all, but it would have been totally inefficient and unworkable, very simply it would not have coped, because yet again they have dived into something without understanding it or having the knowledge to make it work.

One of the mysteries is that on the change of government and the demise of the Home Information Pack, there was no crying from anyone that they had lost a lot of money. All the advertising that had taken place to sell the product these companies had produced, all the set up costs, were absorbed by somebody. The whole idea was disbanded with little protest though some Corporate Conveyancing Companies remain. Who could have absorbed that? Again I leave it to your discretion.

The licensed conveyancing company is here to stay. When there is an up-turn in the market and the number of transactions, solicitors simply will not cope, there is not enough of them left. As transactions tumbled, many conveyancing solicitors, Licenced Conveyancers, and assistants were laid off. Conveyancing solicitors, despite what the public think, are not well paid and again they are a dying breed. As we speak, pressure is already being put on purchasers who are applying for a mortgage and they are being told, the bank/mortgage lender will not use the local solicitor for the mortgage deed, you have to use a certain Conveyancing Company who will, of course, offer to do your conveyance as well. It makes you weep.

EXPAND CORPORATE ESTATE AGENCY

Now the banks and institutions have been down this route before; back in the '80s they invested millions and millions buying out companies of Estate Agents, it went horribly wrong, they couldn't make Estate Agency work. A few tried to save their investment and almost every single one that has survived, survived because it was estate agents who ran them, not bankers or accountants, or financial services people, often from the corporate world but with an understanding of the Estate Agency business. These people proved it could be done and especially in the south of England. So just suppose, the corporate community involved in money relating to the housing market thought it would be a good idea if corporate expansion could take place into estate agency yet again, further their control and ability to sell their financial products, how would you do it? Would you pay vast amounts of money to buy out estate agents' businesses, which until October 2007 were profitable? Well no, they have already been down that route and felt the pain, so they don't want to do that again. Why not make them unprofitable?

Perhaps the easiest way to get market share for the corporate estate agent is very simply to stop people buying houses. Effectively banks' changing lending criteria to a requirement of 30% for a deposit was to do that. It is difficult to find the housing transactions for the years 2009/2010 but my understanding is that residential transactions dropped to something like 600,000.

It is very difficult to find out how many Estate Agency branches closed, or how many Estate Agents jobs were lost. Nobody seems to think that it is important, despite the fact that buying a house is deemed to be such an important transaction in peoples' lives. 'Trained people' who would look after you during this transaction were losing their jobs in droves. It is stated that in 2008 from approximately a total of 80,000 people employed in Estate Agency, a minimum of 32,000 lost their jobs. Many Estate Agents offices closed and many Estate Agency owners lost nearly everything and yet the media seem to think this is of no consequence, as they hardly report anything about it. Corporate closures were relatively few; some corporate bosses indicated that the offices they closed were poor performers in any event. Supported by banks and venture capitalists, they were able to keep going, when the small man could not. When the market revives, they will be there with less competition and ability to expand. One large corporate firm announced in 2011 that it was taking on 1,500 staff. To the Real Estate Agent it was an indication that the brakes on mortgage lending would start to slacken slightly and sure enough within the next 6/12 months, transactions started to rise as mortgage rates became more affordable for those people with a reasonable deposit.

You will say that the Banks demanding a 30% deposit was to improve the security on the properties on which they lend. The trouble with that argument, is that it immediately reduced the security of their existing loans, as it reduced the values of the properties that they had already made loans on. The security argument does not hold water. We have already seen that if banks change their lending criteria, they affect values, and could have effected prices by the reduction of the multiple, as they did in the late '80s, creating negative equity. Instead, they insisted on a 30% deposit overnight, houses became much less saleable as it took the first time buyer, the life blood of the market, out of the market. If estate agents cannot sell houses they go out of business. The overheads stay the same, geared to a certain level of business but the income more than halved. Would be vendors initially still wanted to sell, but no one could buy exacerbating the agent's problem. The proportion of corporate owned Estate Agents offices, against privately owned increased dramatically over that short period of time. Over the years 2008/2009, transaction numbers, the means by which Estate Agents make profit , not house prices, dropped to such a level that overheads simply could not be supported. Was it a deliberate ploy to reduce the numbers of Estate Agents? Was it really necessary to change the lending criteria in such a way when there was always going to be a demand for the product as people have to have somewhere to live and therefore a lenders money is secure. The take up of the Help to Buy scheme on new build has proved the demand and affordability of the public is and was there. Was the credit crunch used as the excuse to introduce the requirement of the 30% deposit in the name of propriety, in order to kill the housing market and with it many estate agents' businesses and jobs.

They wouldn't do that would they! However, that was the result and given their track record on mortgage broking/surveying and their continuing attempts to gain the conveyancing market, I wouldn't put it past them. The effect of the 30% deposit requirement certainly had a spin off benefit to the corporate cause. In 2010 with transaction levels at a minimum, a remarkable article was published in The Negotiator (virtually the only surviving Estate Agency paper at the time) saying that independent estate agents could not survive off current levels of transactions, fees etc. The author was the former Managing Director/Chairman of Countrywide. It was as if he was ringing the final death knell. Many agents may have read the article and felt inclined to give up. Unless we could raise our fees we were unlikely to survive and there was little chance of that.

In the same title in May 2011, a smiling Mr Newberry of LSL Solutions, the owner of Reeds Rains and Your Move and other brands of estate agents owned by various banks and venture capitalists, reported that he was looking to expand with 1,500 new staff. Yet in the same magazine in August 2010, whilst group profits were £19.7 million, the estate agency business made an underlying profit of £2.9 million. If you allow 500 offices (the figure would be more at the time) it is a profit of £5800 per office. Wow, that's a lot, those estate agents really make a lot of money don't they! Still, it is better than the loss of £0.8 million made the previous year. Yet they were virtually paid to acquire the loss making Halifax Estate Agencies from Lloyds Bank and continue to acquire independent agents to this day. Why, on those profit margins?'

According to the online news site Moneypenny 'what Sheila Manchester does not know about the Property industry is not worth knowing' Sheila is now the editor of the Negotiator, but she wrote in October 2013:

'but there's no denying that the residential property industry is going through a period of immense change and much is being lost. The initial dramatic drop in housing transactions in 2008-9 certainly cleared out many of the less professional-aka cowboy-agents, which was a good thing but the longevity of this latest 'global-realignment' which has brought about the demise of many of our long established firms is a sad thing.' and later 'every week we see news of mergers and acquisitions, losing names that have been around for decades, when the portfolio is absorbed, but thankfully, saving names where the buyer operates an umbrella brand. One such corporate is Countrywide.' The thrust of the article then became about letting businesses but they are acquiring Sales Estate Agencies as well. In 2015 Countrywide was reported as announcing an increase in its financing facilities from £150 million to £250 million provided by its banking syndicate of Abbey National Treasury Services, AIB Group (UK) Barclays, HSBC, Lloyds and NatWest.

Countrywide's Chief Financial Officer stated 'We are pleased that our existing banking partners continue to support us and we are able to continue our strategy for growth, both organically and through acquisitions.' Yet for the same year it reported a 4% increase in income but a 37% drop in operating profits after a 'decline in estate agency and lettings profitability.' It is of course interesting to note the list of mortgage providers providing the financial backing to expand, but of more interest is why are they expanding into a business in which they are making so little profit.

The businesses they are acquiring no doubt like most agencies outside of the south-east, and like their new corporate masters, have struggled through the years since the credit crunch, had to diversify into residential lettings and perhaps are gratefully salvaging something from the difficult trading circumstances they continue to find themselves in. Yet why are the Corporates continuing to purchase barely profitable estate agencies when their own estate agency businesses are making so little?

Estate Agents need a certain number of transactions to be profitable and although things have improved, they still need an easing of lending criteria, equal to say of those buying a new build to bring levels back to those of pre credit crunch, and the people who can do that are the same lenders supporting the ever expanding corporate estate agents.

Am I suggesting that mortgage lending has been deliberately held back to depress the housing market to aid further corporate expansion and control of estate agency? That when the Corporates and their Institutional backers deem they have enough control they will change the lending criteria to allow transaction levels to rise making their existing businesses and the ones they have acquired profitable again, but on a huge scale. Am I suggesting that to achieve this they have deliberately hindered the aspirations of home ownership and moving home of millions of the British Public.

I Am Not Sure. They Wouldn't Do That Would They? Of Course Not The Idea Is Madness!

They Wouldn't,
Would They?